# The Ghostwalker File

by

## Kevin Robinson

– The Ghostwalker File –

**Copyright © 2012 Kevin Robinson**
P.O. Box 522617 - Marathon Shores, FL 33052
ghostwalkerfile@gmail.com
**10 9 8 7 6 5 4 3 2 1**

– Kevin Robinson –

# Dedication & Gratitude

Eighteen years after my three Stick Foster mysteries came out in hardback, years after even the paperback editions went out of print, long after my fiction muse flew off to an island of its own, and just after turning 60 (That's 89 in quadriplegic years!), I suddenly **had** to write another novel. When the story opening occurred to me, I actually laughed. A baby boy, abandoned in a cardboard box west of Miami near the Miccosukee Indian Reservation, adopted and raised by the tribe, who grows up to be an architect? Really? Certain it was an aberration, and that my right mind would return if I actually attempted to hammer something out on the word processor, I gave the idea a half-hearted sit-down. The story poured out, filled with interesting people I wish I really knew in real life. Where do such stories come from? Writers have been asked that question throughout history, and no one really knows, but this story wouldn't have happened without the loving support of a handful of real people who chose to believe in a gimpy old has-been writer who decided to charge off like Don Quixote and see what the latest improbable quest was all about.

*The Ghostwalker File* is dedicated to the woman who holds my heart and soul in her gentle hands, who knows me longer and better than anyone else, and who loves me fiercely, every day, just because. To Ellie Apuzzo, my Lady Love, thank you! Thank you for reading, for editing, and for all the wonderful fleshing-out ideas that brought this story's heart and soul to the fore. Most of all, thank you for the miracle of love.

My sincerest thanks also to those other daring few loved ones and friends who interrupted their busy lives to read the manuscript and provide extremely helpful feedback. Elizabeth Moon, one of my favorite authors, calls her first readers "Alpha readers," but knowing that reading my prose is probably nothing like reading hers, my Alpha squad is all-the-more precious! Thanks to my amazing daughter, Melissa, my great friend Alicia Milan, my budding architect and very hip nephew, Taylor Maine, my former collaborator on *GETTING REAL: The Road to Personal Redemption*, Dick Todd, and my dear friend and accomplished architectural engineer, Bill Graham. Having friends who not only give their precious time, but who also aren't afraid to speak truth to you is a priceless writer's boon.

To Joshua Bilmes and Lou Aronica, two publishing industry pros, thank you for the generous gift of time, and for your very helpful advice. And my hardy thanks to Dr. Lewis Mehl-Madrona, whose amazing book *Healing the Mind through the Power of Story* helped me recognize and appreciate the core value of my story and its unique characters. His willingness to write the introduction to *The Ghostwalker File* was a gracious gift, and proof, yet again, that community is where you find it.

And last, but most certainly not least, my thanks to a fellow author who made time to read this book and who, line by line, saved me from myself. For an old adopted guy of unknown origins to suddenly begin writing about a contemporary Native American community in south Florida struck me as the height of hubris. I was ignorant on the subject, yet the words poured out. (Story of my life... ) Enter Pamela Dawes Tambornino, author of one of the most moving and informative memoirs I've ever read: *Maggie's Story: Teachings of a Cherokee Healer*. Pamela is a proud and talented Wolf Clan member of the Cherokee Nation, an English professor at Haskell Indian Nations University, and her knowledge and insight about matters Native American, as well as about the craft of writing, helped me achieve whatever reality there might be in the rich cultural backdrop for *The Ghostwalker File*. Thank you, Pam!

And, of course, this is fiction. Any character's resemblance to anybody in the real world is purely coincidental. Any and all inaccuracies that might remain in this work of fiction are on my head alone.

– The Ghostwalker File –

# Table of Contents

Prologue ............................................................................. 1
Chapter 1: Membership Has its Privileges ...................... 5
Chapter 2: School Spirit..................................................... 9
Chapter 3: Summer of Love............................................. 12
Chapter 4: A Hero's Welcome ......................................... 17
Chapter 5: Swamp Things................................................ 22
Chapter 6: Parkour Brothers............................................ 26
Chapter 7: Meanwhile, Back at the Ranch .................... 29
Chapter 8: He's Leaving Home ....................................... 33
Chapter 9: Hot Town ....................................................... 36
Chapter 10: Property Management ............................... 39
Chapter 11: History in the Making................................. 42
Chapter 12: Three Degrees of Separation...................... 46
Chapter 13: The Doctor Will See You Now................... 50
Chapter 14: Panoramic Views ......................................... 55
Chapter 15: BFF................................................................ 60
Chapter 16: The Man in the Mirror................................ 64
Chapter 17: The Ghost in the Machine ......................... 68
Chapter 18: In for a Penny............................................... 72
Chapter 19: Reverse Engineering.................................... 78
Chapter 20: Knock Three Times ..................................... 82
Chapter 21: Fit for a Queen ............................................. 87
Chapter 22: A Picture's Worth a Thousand Words ......91
Chapter 23: Trip the Limelight Fandango ..................... 95

Chapter 24: Ding Dong .................................................. 100

Chapter 25: Parting Ways ............................................. 105

Chapter 26: Family Ties ............................................... 109

Chapter 27: Hollywood Nights ..................................... 114

Chapter 28: Dancing with the Devil ............................. 119

Chapter 29: Personal Space ......................................... 123

Chapter 30: Room and Board ...................................... 127

Chapter 31: Space Station Miami ................................ 131

Chapter 32: Lost and Found ........................................ 136

Chapter 33: Repercussions .......................................... 142

Chapter 34: Up the Tree Without a Paddle ................. 147

Chapter 35: An Ah-Ha Moment ................................... 151

Chapter 36: Reality Check Please ................................ 155

Chapter 37: High Flying Paranoia ................................ 159

Chapter 38: Hustle and Bustle ..................................... 164

Chapter 39: The Corporate Shuffle .............................. 169

Chapter 40: Special Delivery ........................................ 173

Chapter 41: Behind the Scenes .................................... 177

Chapter 42: Loose Ends ................................................ 180

Chapter 43: *Mi Casa es Su Casa* ................................ 185

Chapter 44: Grand Openings ....................................... 189

Chapter 45: More Loose Ends ..................................... 193

Chapter 46: The Heart and Soul of the Hunter .......... 200

Epilogue ........................................................................ 206

About the Author ........................................................ 209

## Prologue

My name is Sean McKnight, and I used to live on a tiny island in the middle of the Florida Keys. My home office windows looked out over the ocean, and the sound of palm fronds rustling in the warm tropical breezes was the music to which I worked. Otherwise, it was very quiet there in Paradise. Most of my neighbors were snowbirds, so I might see them once or twice a year, and that was fine with me. I've always felt that people are best when kept at arm's length.

I'm a freelance headhunter. The way my business usually works is that I receive a call from an individual small business owner, a corporate HR representative, or even the head of a government department of some sort or another. The client has a pretty good idea of the kind of employee they're looking for and the guidelines I'm given are, more often than not, pretty straightforward. So with the Internet being what it is, and my 20-some years of discovering ways to use--if not abuse--the worldwide web being very well honed, finding a good match is usually a simple matter of connecting the digital dots. The money's good, I can--and do--work from anywhere, and the job leaves me plenty of time to pursue my hobby as an anti-social anthropological voyeur. I used to call myself a scientist instead of a voyeur, but after reading a self-help Kindle book called *Getting Real: the Road to Personal Redemption*, I've been working hard to eliminate the bullshit and the drama in my life. As a reminder to myself, I bought two little signs, one for my desk and the other for the dash of my car, that say: "Figure it out and do it!"

On the job, I hunt people down, usually by their educational and employment background. Before I even consider talking to them on the phone, I learn everything that I can possibly learn about them. My clients don't like surprises, and repeat business depends largely on details that often go far beyond technical skills. A great computer programmer, for example, is relatively easy to find in this day and age, but finding one who doesn't have issues with authority, situational ethics, and/or basic social skill quirks, well, not so much. My clients are primarily interested in a "good fit," a team player who's looking for a home, one who won't likely be looking to trade up any time soon just because they can. So in my day job, social anthropology is a core science resource, but what sparks my passion are the individuals I sometimes come across who have mad skills, matched by even madder personal quirks. They are quirky to the extreme, they are lone wolves; and, metaphorically at least, I collect them like butterflies. My display case is an old cigar box I picked up in Key West, and instead of straight pins, I use computer thumb drives to memorialize my discoveries.

There are thirteen thumb drives in my cigar box, and aside from smelling good, they each have their number written on them with an indelible felt-tip pen. Drives one through twelve are all fascinating people, each of whom provided me with weeks, or even months, of thoroughly enjoyable research. They are case studies in human uniqueness, and I am in awe of each one of them...though, in good conscience, I would probably never recommend them to one of my regular clients as a stable, long term employee. Other than in Internet pictures, I have never seen them. Neither have I spoken to them in person nor by phone. I have not exchanged emails, nor have I corresponded with them in any way. I may know more about them than anyone else on the planet, perhaps more than they realize about themselves, but we are strangers. That always seemed like the only right thing for me to do.

– The Ghostwalker File –

## Chapter 1: Membership Has its Privileges

"Almost every journey," according to Grandmother Renee Persons, "begins with a misstep. We are, after all, very human beings. We are born seeking, but more often than not we must learn what to seek for. And that, my dear child, takes time."

John D. Ghostwalker got his undergraduate degree in Lawrence, Kansas, beginning at Haskell and finishing up at KU. He went on to receive a Masters in Architectural Design from Georgia Tech, a PhD from Florida International University, and went to work shortly thereafter for an upscale Miami firm called Jacobs & Associates. Tribal elders called him "John Doe" at first. He was discovered in a cardboard box along the shoulder of Route 41 in the Florida Everglades. The high school boys and girls who stopped their pickup truck to investigate the weathered cardboard box near the turn-off to their part time jobs at the Miccosukee Museum Village noted that the only possible explanation for Baby John Doe not having been gobbled up by one of the myriad alligators in the nearby canal was the overwhelming stench of his diaper. The kids were instructed by the adults to clean the abandoned baby up and see to feeding him while they waited for more elders to arrive. Over the next several months, John Doe became "Johnny D," and a strangely unscripted schedule of babysitting found the blond-haired infant being passed around to nearly every household in the nearby neighborhood, as well as frequent migrations to other predominantly Miccosukee neighborhoods along the highway that is called Tamiami Trail by the locals.

The General Council officers of the Miccosukee tribe were not officially notified, and it was generally held that the less official, but more traditional, community elders, perhaps being influenced somewhat by the wives among them, put off deciding what to do with the little lost white man for a bit too long. Impromptu neighborhood gatherings could and did happen anywhere, at anyone's house or in anyone's backyard. But when people felt the spirit move them to discuss important matters, they were irresistibly drawn to Grandmother Renee's little cottage, where they packed into her tiny living room. So, at about the same time someone finally suggested calling Miami-Dade County's child welfare services office, others vigorously objected, and everyone migrated to Grandmother Renee's house.

"How will we explain our delay?" one neighbor asked.

"How can we prove anything we might say about this child?" said the lady cradling little Johnny in her arms as she sat in the old rocking chair next to Grandmother Renee's overstuffed wingback. "And, besides, there's been nothing in the news about anyone missing a baby."

The idea of a protracted investigation by non-tribal officials appealed to no one at all. Grandmother Renee watched the ladies faces closely, smiled warmly and shook her head. She reached out for the tiny child, and could not fail to notice the unspoken reluctance that accompanied the woman's immediate compliance.

"You have a hold on us, don't you?" she whispered to the baby boy as she gazed curiously into his blue-green eyes. "Why does your wind blow you our way, child?"

Johnny's face broke into one of those baby grins that seems unnaturally mature and that sometimes precipitates a burp. The roomful of tightly compacted Miccosukee neighbors held their breath as if he might respond. He rewarded them with a giggle, and promptly began playing with his toes.

"He came to us for a reason," Grandmother Renee said finally. "And like most good things, I'm afraid we must wait some before we know what that reason is."

Everyone nodded solemnly. Some things are never divined scientifically, but then *faith is the substance of things hoped for, the evidence of things not seen*. There is no record indicating even a single objection to Johnny D's unofficial and unorthodox adoption into the tribe.

By all accounts, little John Doe was extremely healthy and, by any standard, an easy baby. He seldom fussed, never had tantrums, and transitioned from household to household with no signs of distress. And while everyone just seemed to enjoy holding the child, when left alone, he entertained himself with remarkable contentment. He showed no signs of separation anxiety when it came time for kindergarten; in fact, he simply got up from the breakfast table, gathered up his hand-me-down backpack, and walked three blocks to the elementary school on the very first day. No one in the household ever saw him leave, and by the time his "mom" searched the house and followed his trail, Johnny D was already sitting quietly at his desk drawing pictures in his tablet while the harried kindergarten teacher dealt with half a dozen weepy and agitated children. Grade school records indicate that John was an excellent, if somewhat seemingly unfocussed student. He apparently completed his assignments promptly, and developed the disconcerting habit of disappearing whenever he—not the teacher—decided he was finished. His third grade teacher at the tribal school made this note in his file:

*"Johnny is always obedient, is never disruptive or late to class, and is always kind and thoughtful towards others, often going out of his way to help other children. I must confess, however, that I have a difficult time actually documenting his coming and going. Johnny is either here, or he is not."*

This oft-repeated observation, though worded differently each time, led eventually to his surname, and if John D. Ghostwalker showed up at one's home for a meal, he was always welcomed. If he did not show up, one could only assume that he was eating with another household. Neither adults nor peers ever gave his whereabouts a second thought. While everyone gladly accepted corporate responsibility for the lad, no one seemingly took specific responsibility for him, but there is no indication that Ghostwalker, himself, cared a wit about any of it. He was loved, and by all appearances, he thrived on it.

Be that as it may, John Ghostwalker is living proof that there is a vast difference between being discovered and discovering one's self.

## Chapter 2: School Spirit

By junior high school, Johnny Ghostwalker was something of a local tribal legend. His peculiarities (if not his comings and goings) were becoming more evident. John was a died-in-the-wool hunter-gatherer, but his prey was very non-traditional. He was jokingly referred to as the tribe's official recycling officer because wherever he went, John collected trash. He seemed fondest of paper and cardboard, but he didn't discriminate. These materials never made it to the county's blue recycling bins, but when they did occasionally reappear, it was in the form of classroom and/or school art or science fair projects. It is commonly reported (though somewhat tongue-and-cheek) that his $7^{th}$ grade history project not only garnered him an A+ grade, but was fabricated entirely out of the cardboard box in which he'd first arrived at the Miccosukee reservation. The fact that the project was an exquisitely detailed replica of that same museum village just made the story better.

– The Ghostwalker File –

Junior high school is the place where children begin to differentiate between themselves. They strive to be noticed, or to go unnoticed. They give each other nicknames, sometimes out of respect, sometimes not so much. Boys notice girls, and girls notice being noticed. Johnny became John in the teacher's notes, but to his classmates he was "the Ghost." Classroom teachers referred to his "vanishing act" more with whimsical interest than with concern, and the gym teacher noted his growing affinity toward gymnastics with this anecdote:

*"I was introducing the 7th grade boys to the gymnastics equipment when I noticed that John Ghostwalker was no longer present. I asked the other students where he had gone, and was answered with puzzled head shaking until one student looked up and pointed. John was calmly looking down at us from the gym ceiling, and when I told him to climb back down the heavy rope, he did so effortlessly. The boy also took to the horse and the parallel bars like he'd been born on them."*

Yet no teacher ever referred to John as a show-off. He neither sought attention, nor reacted appreciatively to receiving it. Their notes always hinted at the boy's uniqueness in one way or another. One teacher called it his "wonder of discovery," and another noted that Ghostwalker seemed "drawn" to certain activities, particularly those involving drawing and constructing models. One of his art projects was featured in the tribal newspaper. It dwarfed the other students' projects, not only in size and scope, but in its artistic vision as well.

*"Pictured above is one of the projects from the Carter Middle School's Spring Art Show. The massive mobile was created by John Ghostwalker, a 7th grader, and was constructed from discarded wire coat hangers, used fishing line, and 48 empty oil cans. Recycled finishing nails were used to punch holes in the center of each screw-off cap, and then tied to the end of the fishing line after it was fed through the hole before the cap was screwed back on. This ingenious creation was perfectly balanced and spun slowly and gracefully overhead throughout the*

*evening. The talented young man modestly fielded questions from those in attendance, including many having to do with who had helped him design and build the piece. He always insisted that he had 'just thought it up,' and neither his classmates nor his art teacher seemed to doubt this. This reporter's question about whether Mr. Ghostwalker thought his art might someday be hung in the Miami airport terminal drew a sheepish grin and a typical 7th grade response: 'Not likely.'"*

Amongst themselves, his teachers marveled at John's ability to appear perpetually distracted. What they all initially assumed was note-taking, turned out to be very involved doodling, often consisting of unique buildings or even entire cityscapes with elaborate urban highway designs. And yet, to their never-ending amazement, not one of them ever caught him unprepared to correctly answer a question about their lessons. John completed assignments and exams long before his classmates, but never once let on. He always kept himself busy at his desk until other classmates began turning in their work. His classroom exams, as well as the various standardized tests he took, underscored the obvious. John Ghostwalker was an exceptional student.

## Chapter 3: Summer of Love

Becky Deacon was a classmate of John's that year, and by the end of term, classmates and teachers had noticed her interest in young Ghostwalker. Becky's mother was Miccosukee and her father was a Seminole, and so summer vacation threatened her romantic designs. The Deacon home in Hollywood, Florida was located in a modest, middle class neighborhood, not far from the Seminole Hard Rock Hotel and Casino where Mr. Deacon was employed. But, as luck would have it, Becky's aunt and uncle on her mom's side lived in John's neighborhood. Her folks were a bit surprised when Becky turned down her invitation to attend band camp at the University of Miami that summer, but they were secretly pleased when she asked if she could visit her aunt instead. Sometimes kids can seem a little slow to embrace the true value of family, and can at times seem more interested in their cell phones than in their roots. Where their family is, the heart is, so Becky's folks were thrilled.

Three notable changes began for John "the Ghost" Ghostwalker that year. First, he discovered money. He knew what it was before this, of course, but since he had, in effect, dozens of "parents," his every need had always been met, almost magically. Hand-me-down clothes, toys and school supplies always appeared when needed; and unlike some of his peers, he showed no interest in having the "latest" anything. The story goes that John just walked into Nathan Blackfeather's backyard shop on a Monday morning that summer and went to work. By that evening when the mechanic arrived home from his day job at the Macco shop on Krome Avenue in Homestead, the place was unrecognizable.

"Well, well, my young tinkerer," Nate said with a smile, "what have you been up to this time?" Nate and his family probably saw more of Ghostwalker than most of the tribe because the boy had been drawn to the mechanic's workshop years before. But where his activities might have previously been classified as creative play, this was definitely something different altogether. Every tool was cleaned, polished, and neatly arranged, either in one of the shop's tool boxes, or on one of the freshly painted white pegboard wall units. The large, rusty bench vice had been wire brushed and lubricated with white lithium grease so that it opened and closed smoothly and quietly...something it had never done before. The work bench was empty for the first time in decades, and had also been painted white. The shop floor was swept and mopped, and the windows which had previously let in less light than the tin wall panels, were gleaming like the ones those birds fly into on the television commercials. And, somehow, the place just looked bigger.

"Just cleaning up a bit, sir," John answered. "Oh, and I finished rebuilding Benny Cairn's carburetor."

"And how did you manage that?" Nate asked as he searched the shop for the now missing unit.

"It's back in Benny's car," the boy said, reading the unasked question on Nate's face. "I took the instructions out of the rebuild kit you had, and I wrote out all the numbered parts on the back of that head gasket box over there as I took it apart. Then I put each piece by the number on the box as I took it apart, replaced all the parts that the kit had in it, cleaned the rest with a toothbrush and solvent, and then went backwards through the numbers and put it back together."

"I'll be damned," was all Nate could say as he retrieved the gasket box from a nearby shelf and looked over John's numbered drawing. "Why did you lay it all out this way? Doesn't the blow-up diagram in the rebuild kit show all the same stuff?"

"Well, yes it does, but that diagram doesn't tell you what order the pieces are supposed to be assembled in, so I was afraid I might do something backwards when it came time to put it back together."

"I'll be damned," Nate said again as he grabbed Benny's keys off the newly whitewashed pegboard by the shop door and headed outside.

John followed him quietly, but looked away when the car roared instantly to life. Knowing that the fuel pump would have needed ten or twenty seconds to refill the line and the empty carburetor, Nate simply stated the obvious: "You already fired it up."

"I just had to know," the thirteen year old admitted.

Nate just laughed out loud, and instead of being a proud parent, he was just one of many. That summer, in large part due to his new assistant, tribe members and friends alike saw their cars and trucks repaired in days rather than weeks. For his part, John Ghostwalker opened a checking account and became a catalog shopper. His first purchase was a small draftsman's kit in a wooden box with a brass latch. He redesigned an outside pocket on his hand-me-down backpack, and carried his new treasure with him everywhere he went.

John's second change that year was his hair. For reasons he never offered and no one ever asked, he let it grow out, and began tying the wavy yellow mane into a pony tail with a piece of used shoestring. The shoestring was replaced at the insistence of his new shadow, Becky Deacon. "It's a 'scrunchy,'" she explained as she wrapped the black stretchy band several times around his pony tail, "and this one's good luck."

Junior high aged girls notice not being noticed just as much as they notice being noticed. Maybe more. But they also know what to do about it, and Becky was no exception. She set to the task of getting John Ghostwalker to notice her with great determination, and no small amount of dismay. He hadn't been nicknamed for naught, and while every other teenager in the community hung out, bummed rides to the mall, and planned group dates at the movie theater, the Ghost proved to Becky that he was nothing like every other teenager. It is one thing to be a ghost when no one is particularly concerned about where you are, but that was no longer true for young Ghostwalker, and he adapted to this with his third change: a total reorganization of his work schedule at Nate's shop. Although Nate seldom saw the boy that month, the work always got done. Not that proof was needed, but Nate's electric bill confirmed what he already knew: John was working nights.

Grandmother Renee's old wooden rocking chair obviously held a special place in John's life. From an early age, when he'd still needed a boost to climb into it, he just showed up to rock and listen silently to Grandmother Renee's voice as she told him stories about his Miccosukee family. When John showed up more often that summer, and sometimes nodded off to sleep in the chair, Grandmother Renee smiled knowingly, poked her left toe under the closest rocker, and gently kept the chair going until John woke up, hugged her, and slipped away.

Becky was no match for the boy who wasn't there. When they met, he was cordial and treated her the same way he treated all of his other brothers and sisters. This, of course, was worse than being ignored; but the truth was, they seldom met. After a couple weeks of randomly dropping by various families homes at dinner time, and being relentlessly teased by the other teenagers for her constant inquiries as to the whereabouts of the village ghost, Becky gave up and went back to her life in the city.

## Chapter 4: A Hero's Welcome

    High school brought out more of John Ghostwalker's not-so-hidden talents. Shop classes, auto mechanics, and drafting were givens, but unlike most boys who gravitated toward those disciplines, John also excelled in history, math and physics. To the coach's great dismay, the boy politely refused to join the gymnastics team, but was seen practicing on the equipment whenever it was not in use and he was not in class. John came and went as inconspicuously as always, and because so many of his classmates were adoptive brothers and sisters, it just meant that they thought little or nothing about it. But in High School, even counting the Seminole students, Native Americans were no longer the majority. John began to understand that non-Native Americans weren't always kind to people who were different. He was often ridiculed mildly for being illusive and nerdy, but was disturbed far more to see and hear non-Native attitudes about his fellow tribe members ... bigotry he never faced because he didn't look like them.

"Why do some non-Natives seem to dislike people who are different, Grandmother?" John asked one day after school. "Some of them say mean things that make no sense."

"We all do that sometimes, child," Grandmother Renee said, "and it usually happens when we are afraid. Fear can arise from, and give voice to, our ignorance, and ignorance can lead to stories that have no power to heal. What have I taught you about ignorance?"

"Meet ignorance with diligent study and with respectful silence," John answered.

"It is not always easy," she said, tussling his hair with her hand, "but it is almost always right."

John grew quite proficient on his new personal computer, and one of his first email messages was a "thank you" note to the Miccosukee Resort & Casino's management and staff, whose annual tradition was to provide free laptops to the tribe's incoming high school freshmen. Shortly thereafter, John discovered kipkay.com, where he learned even more about electronics, particularly more about how to salvage parts and pieces out of one discarded item and use them to create another item. For example, he discovered that the broken Barbie doll he'd lifted off the top of someone's curbside trash can--thinking he might patch it up and give it to a different neighbor kid--had a digital camera built into it. Kip Kay showed him exactly how to turn it into a functioning security camera. This information was right up John's alley, and the world-wide web was crammed full of it. He carried his laptop everywhere in a newer used backpack, along with a growing number of light and compact tools he had purchased with his weekly paychecks.

Despite this successful entry into the world of microchip technology, John still showed no interest in owning a cell phone, but his ability to fix complicated equipment was just another growing facet of his reputation. Late in his freshman year, he overheard the school's head custodial engineer requesting a service call for the building's security camera system. A note in his permanent record indicates that Ghostwalker strolled back into the office an hour later and informed one of the secretaries that the cameras had been repaired, and that the service call could be cancelled.

On those rare occasions when he missed the bus, the boy simply walked home. If a neighbor stopped and offered him a lift, he accepted it graciously, but otherwise, the five and a half mile trek didn't seem to bother him a bit. It was during one of these long hikes home that John first met Dan Stone. John had heard about Stone, a weathered old Native American who had returned from Vietnam in 1971 with a substance abuse issue and a perpetual cough which he blamed on Agent Orange. He was harmless enough, and the tribal police department looked after him when they could, and drove him to and from the VA hospital when his health issues took their annual nose dive each February. He lived somewhere in the vicinity of the Everglades Fish Camp, just a couple of miles west of the Miccosukee casino, but no one was sure just where and how the homeless vet made do.

The fish camp was closed when John Ghostwalker came past on his way home from school, and the black SUV with tinted windows and purple L.E.D. lights under the wheel wells and the running boards looked out of place in the gravel parking lot. A few yards beyond the tricked out truck, Dan Stone was trying in vain to fight off the four young thugs who had chosen to hassle him. Between punches, kicks and profane insults, their laughter seemed to be the only thing keeping Stone in the fight. The old man had been drinking, and was hopelessly outnumbered, but somehow his indignation and his combat training kept him on his feet. John quietly opened the truck's passenger door, reached in, and slipped the shifter into neutral. Seconds later, he seemed to appear out of nowhere and calmly addressed the four young men.

"Is that your truck?" he said, pointing back towards the slowly moving machine. "Cool lights."

"What's it to you, punk?" said one of them, but the other three were already running back toward the vehicle, and after a backwards glance, the speaker followed them without waiting for an answer. They barely managed to stop the truck, just as its front wheels rolled off the parking lot and onto the narrow wooden dock that ran parallel to the shoreline. The dock boards creaked painfully under the sudden weight as the SUV's engine turned over and the driver eased the vehicle back onto terra firma. That's when the four wannabe gang bangers realized that both the scruffy old homeless man and the long-haired kid were nowhere to be seen.

For the next month, John scoured every garage and backyard shed in every neighborhood he knew his way around. "Do you need this?" "Can I have this?" "Are you gonna throw this away?" For a boy who seldom asked anybody for anything, John proved himself to be a very capable beggar. His tribal family was highly amused and overwhelmingly generous, and many of their non-Native American neighbors gladly pitched in as well. But folks were genuinely taken aback when they realized that the authentic looking "Tribal Workday" posters that showed up everywhere had been created and tacked up by Ghostwalker, not the elders. Be that as it may, along with several off duty tribal police officers, nearly two dozen men showed up on that Saturday with their vehicles, and helped him cart all his newly collected junk down to the fish camp. The men all just grinned, shrugged, and followed his lead when John gathered up an arm load of junk and waded out into the shin-deep swamp water.

All day long they followed his "blueprints" to a tee. By nightfall, Dan Stone's swampy little island had been 'gator-proofed, his plastic paint tarp pole tent had disappeared, and he was the proud owner of a new house. Well, house might be a stretch, but to call it an efficiency bungalow required no exaggeration at all. It had everything including a kitchen sink, and its rain barrel was rigged to supply the sink, the shower, and the recycled marine toilet, all while helping to hold down the ancient and up-side-down fiberglass catamaran hull roof. The "stereo system" came out of an ancient Volkswagen, as did the 6-volt battery that powered it. A series of discarded cell phone solar rechargers would keep the battery charged, at least in good weather, and the speakers were so cleverly hidden that there was no telling where, exactly, the sounds of Classic Rock FM radio came from.

 John had somehow talked the owners of the fish camp into providing Dan with a bag of ice a day, and a water cooler-sized bottle of potable water once a week...all in exchange for Dan's new responsibility as their "night watchman." The little clay garden fireplace vented neatly through the catamaran's twin "centerboard" slots, thanks to a roll of duct tape, a couple of heavy tin funnels, a few feet of repurposed air conditioning duct, and some radiator hose donated by Nate Blackfeather. As darkness fell on the Everglades, the little island teemed with tribal life. Women from the nearest neighborhood showed up with sandwiches and cold drinks, a group of children took it upon themselves to pick up the "yard" and the "garden" while they danced to the sounds of the FM radio, and the men swapped the kind of stories that get passed down for good reason. When Dan Stone looked up from his tiny fireplace, put his arm around John Ghostwalker's shoulder, and said that he felt like he'd finally come home, there wasn't a dry eye in the house.

## Chapter 5: Swamp Things

No one would have ever taken Dan Stone for the mentoring type, but he took John Ghostwalker to heart with great dedication. Even while under the influence, he was profoundly conscious of what the boy had done for him. He was determined to give back, and the only thing he had to share was his experience and his knowledge. With the exception of a teary tale about "the girl who got away," Dan's drunken stories usually began and ended in Vietnam, and the Miccosukee police officers who looked out for him believed less and less of what he told them because the stories seemed to change with each retelling, but for some reason the old vet thought that his war stories were unsuitable for the ghost child. Instead, he would teach John what he knew best: how to survive in the wild.

John accepted Dan's heartfelt offer with honest gratefulness and no small amount of curiosity. Being able to exist, alone on a swampy island, in a snake and alligator infested swamp was no small thing to a teenage boy. He had fished in the Everglades, and grown up watching the ever-present alligators, but despite the stories of tribal history and the demonstrations at the museum village, John was far removed from the reality of living off the land. And even that long-lost tradition took the cooperative diligence of the entire tribe. Dan Stone, a hermit, was an older, under-the-influence Rambo in the eyes of a young boy.

The lessons began in a fairly straightforward manner. John learned to identify and track numerous denizens of the Everglades, including a relative newcomer that was making the news on a regular basis, the Burmese Python. Dan taught him how to set traps and snares, and how to safely dispatch dangerous creatures with only a knife...though it was sometimes lashed to the end of a stout piece of bamboo. And, in honored Native tradition, almost nothing went to waste. What wasn't eaten or skinned and tanned went into a small chicken wire compost bin next to Dan's vegetable/herb garden.

How Dan had ever managed cooking in his plastic tent, John could only guess, but the old vet was an artist in his modest new island kitchen. John was amazed to discover how good snake and alligator tasted when Dan was finished preparing them, and he was moved each time the old man paused in respectful silence after each kill. Drunk or sober, Dan Stone was deeply connected to his roots.

"But how can I ever learn about all the plants out here?" John asked one day. "There are bazillions of them!"

"Ah," said the old vet, "but we only have to learn the edible ones for right now. There are hundreds of thousands of plants around the world, and many are good medicine, especially here in the Glades, but we'll touch on those later. For now, let's stick with stuff we can eat. All around the world, there are only a few thousand edible plants. Of those, we only see a few hundred in our markets, but here in this swamp there are just over a dozen worth memorizing...so that's not so bad, is it?"

"I can do that!" John said hopefully. "Where do we start?"

"Right where I started with my Grandfather; we learn the three P's first: Plant, Place, and Preparation."

And so John learned how to be sure a plant was what he thought it was, how to double check that it was in the right kind of place, getting clean, fresh rather than foul, stagnant water, and only then did he learn how to prepare it for the table.

Like anything else that happened within the tribe, everyone was in the know, and folks talked about Dan Stone's new role as a dedicated mentor and John Ghostwalker's obvious affection for the disenfranchised old vet. The effect the relationship was having on both of them was a topic of joyful gossip, and it had been months since anyone had seen Dan intoxicated in public. No one was naïve enough to believe that Stone was clean and sober, but as Grandmother Renee Persons liked to say: "Every flood begins with one drop of rain."

For John, his new-felt confidence about exploring the Everglades seemed to flow over into other areas of his life. He was, as neighbors often noted, continuing his passage into manhood quite well.

"So, young Ghostwalker," Dan said as they glided towards his little island in an ancient camo-colored canoe, "do you have a girlfriend?"

"No," John answered quickly. "What about you?"

"Almost," Dan said wistfully, a faraway look in his eyes. "When I came back from Nam I was really screwed up, John, and it took me sixteen years just to get up the courage to ask a lady out on a date."

"I take it that it didn't go so smooth," John said.

"Well, I thought it went great. She was incredible! I met her on a visit to the VA Hospital in Miami, I fell madly in love, head over heels as they say, and I felt like I could overcome anything in order to spend my life with her. We just meshed, and felt so comfortable together. When I left her apartment one morning, and she kissed me goodbye, I never imagined that goodbye was, well you know, forever."

"Ouch! How did she drop that bomb?"

"She didn't. I never saw her, nor heard from her again, so if you've heard folks say 'the one that got away,' I guess I talk too much when I'm drunk."

"But you went back to her place, her job? She didn't just disappear?"

"Off the face of the earth, young Ghostwalker. Rosie--or whatever her real name was--disappeared off the face of the earth."

## Chapter 6: Parkour Brothers

During his senior year, on Saturdays when John was finished working for Nate, and on Sundays when he usually had the whole day to himself, he began exploring the urban jungle. He'd usually walk east as far as Krome Avenue and catch the bus that followed Tamiami Trail all the way into Miami where it becomes Southwest 8th Street and runs through Coral Gables and Little Havana into the heart of the Brickell District. There is no telling why Ghostwalker was drawn to this unique neighborhood, but there is no doubt that it captivated him, educated him, and somehow took him in. Sometimes he visited the Main Public Library just to the north. He learned his way around the FIU campus on Brickell Avenue, discovering not only its library, but its Graduate School of Architecture as well. Sometimes he just wandered the streets, where he would pass by more banks and foreign consulate buildings than in almost any other neighborhood in America. There is a mixture of high rise industry and luxury residential property that defies common boundaries, and has earned Brickell the nickname "Manhattan of the South." But wherever his weekend travels might lead him, John always ended up at the same place.

Not to be confused with the Biscayne Bay shoreline Brickell Park, the Allen Morris Brickell Park-- between South Miami Avenue and Southeast 1$^{st}$ Avenue at Southeast 10$^{th}$ Street--was clearly John's home away from home. He bought his scant meals at Perricone's Marketplace & Café, took over a shady park bench, opened up his wooden architect's kit, and sketched countless drawings of nearly everything he saw. No one could have guessed that ten years and three degrees later, those local drawings, as much as anything else that came after, would help him land a job just blocks from where he sat drawing them.

One gorgeous Sunday, while John sat sketching on his least favorite bench (the one sitting directly on Southeast 10$^{th}$ Street, right out in front of God and everyone), he was so taken aback that he dropped his mechanical lead pencil, let his tablet slide off his lap, and rose to his feet where he stood staring open-mouthed as two identical young Latino men simultaneously vaulted over the railing on the elevated Metrorail line that ran north and south just across Southeast 1st Avenue. The look-alikes dropped lightly onto the plexi-glass roofing that covered the street access stairway; then, one after the other, leaped out over the sidewalk, swung neatly around the square metal utility pole, launched onto a tree branch that extended out over the street, and then dropped lightly to the ground directly across Southeast 10$^{th}$ Street from where John stood gawking at them. Both guys looked at him, laughed, and crossed the street. One picked up John's tablet and pen while the other pulled a wrinkled business card out of his back pocket. All three items were handed to him, and before he could fashion a response, the twins said "Check us out!" in unison and darted into the park. He caught a last glimpse of the acrobatic brothers as they scaled a huge bronze sculpture, vaulted onto the roof of Grimpas'

Steakhouse, and disappeared from sight.

The business card said "Miami Parkour and Free-Running Club," and listed Emanuel and Jose Rosario as "Instructors." A website address and a local phone number were displayed, under which the card said "Call for membership info and class schedules." Sometimes we discover our passion, but John Ghostwalker's lifetime passion had just discovered him.

## Chapter 7: Meanwhile, Back at the Ranch

    Winter turned faintly towards spring in the Everglades as it always did, with little of substance to mark the occasion. Life was good. Marion and Nathan Blackfeather's daughter, Rachel, was the apple of her parents' eye. The ten-year-old was bright, funny, and she shared her folks' love of television crime shows...even if the autopsy scenes creeped her out a little. She loved to try and guess who the murderer was, and often puzzled it out before mom and dad.
    Whether it was genuine, or a touch of jealousy towards her ghost brother, Rachel had begun to show interest in Nate's work at the backyard shop. She began asking intelligent questions about her dad's tools, about the various cars and trucks he worked on, and especially about what she could do to help. As far as the last inquiry went, whenever Nate was at a loss about what she might do, John was always quick to suggest a task, and turned out to

be an extremely patient teacher. Under her big brother's tutelage, Rachel not only became a definite asset around the shop, but unlike her dad, she adopted John's penchant for cleanliness and order.

On a Sunday afternoon, while her mom and some neighbor ladies sat visiting around the picnic table, and her dad and his friends settled in to watch the Dolphins' game on TV, Rachel puttered around the workshop. Sunday was the perfect day to sweep out the floor, empty the shop vac and make sure that all her dad's tools were clean and in their proper places. She whistled as she waltzed around with the broom, imagining that she was belle of the ball. As she swept along the back of the shop, she noticed that there were semi-circular scratches below on the left and above to the right of the step ladder which always hung horizontally on the back wall. Her love of puzzles gave her the answer in an instant, and she reached out to her left and pushed downwards on the ladder's wider end. Sure enough, as the ladder's feet swung down towards the floor, scraping lightly against the wall on the way, the top step pivoted upwards toward the plywood boards that covered the rafters.

It was then that Rachel noticed the small cut-out in the edge of the plywood where it met the wall, just a few feet above the top of the now upright ladder. She wondered why she hadn't noticed it before. Then she wondered what was up there. It was an irresistible puzzle for a child who loved puzzles, but when she stepped on the lowest rung, the ladder tilted suddenly to the right, and she stumbled back awkwardly. The ladder's rubber-covered feet hung several inches above the floor, and there was a heavy bolt, washer and nut securing the ladder's left side to the wall. The plot thickened. She could get a wrench and undo the nut, but some puzzler's instinct told her that there was another way. That's when she noticed the faint drag marks in the dust on the floor and the old piece of pine 4" X 4" nearby which had obviously caused them. When she kicked the timber sideways along the wall until it was directly under the ladder, the space between it and the rubber ladder feet was just enough to slip a playing card into...maybe.

This time she went up the ladder like a cat, and peeked up into the hole above. Aside from the little light slipping past her that faintly illuminated the back wall near her head, everything else up there was pitch black. Rachel climbed back down, walked to the open bay where her father's trouble light hung from its retracting spool, grabbed it with growing excitement and anticipation, and headed back up the ladder. The cord ran out just short of the hole in the make-shift ceiling, so Rachel leaned back out of the way and pointed the light up as best she could. Her scream brought all the ladies outside to their feet, and her mother burst through the screen door just as the shop light shot back into its spooler and shattered, spraying tiny glass shards everywhere. Rachel was nowhere to be seen, but her ear-splitting demands that someone call the police already had several ladies on their cell phones. Marion found her frantic daughter flat on her back, on the floor, flailing like a turtle on crack, desperate to right itself, but making no progress.

By the time the tribal police officer arrived, the chaos was, for the most part, all over. Her mother continued to comfort her while Nate explained what had happened to the officer, but Rachel kept interrupting, asking "Are you sure? Are you sure?"

"Yes, honey," her father said again, "we're sure."

For the next three hours, everyone in the neighborhood who was physically able took a turn climbing the ladder with a camera or a cell phone. They all agreed as how, on first glance, the young Blackfeather girl might think that she'd discovered the lair of a serial killer, what with the walls and the ceiling of the hidden room covered as they were with drawings and such, but as they compared their digital photos, and discussed the room's ingenuity, the adults were more chagrinned at their own failure to notice the obvious.

"I wonder how long John's lived up there?" was an oft-repeated question, but even Nate and Marion had no clue.

— The Ghostwalker File —

"Do you think he's lonely?" asked the wife of one of the elder's. "I'd hate to have him thinking that none of us want him...just because we always thought he was with someone else."

"He always seems happy," replied another neighborhood mom, "always so content and stable, don't you think?"

Everyone nodded their agreement.

"Just look at his drawings," said the police officer as he drank his second cup of Marion's coffee and poured over the pictures he'd taken with the department's digital Nikon, "and all the models he's built out of trash. He's really quite remarkable."

At a little after 9:00 p.m., when John Ghostwalker returned from his third Parkour class in Brickell, he found half the neighborhood sitting around in the Blackfeather's backyard, discussing their favorite ghost child. They fell silent when he stepped into the yellow circle of back porch light, but seconds later, the questions poured out like flood waters, and so it was after midnight (and a dozen heartfelt invitations) that John finally climbed up his "secret" ladder, and, thanks to the Barbie cam he'd installed in a tiny hole in his plywood floor, watched the video record of Rachel's panic and the shop light's demise. Then, with the smile still on his face, he collapsed into the exquisitely designed hammock bed he had fabricated out of a discarded mullet net, and fell into a deep, contented sleep.

– Kevin Robinson –

## Chapter 8: He's Leaving Home

There are a host of good reasons why so many Native American young people transition into college by way of Haskell Indian Nations University, and long before his high school graduation day arrived, John had determined to follow that tradition. For a number of reasons, his adopted family was, once again, quite surprised by their non-Native son. First, his grades, his standardized test scores, and his letters of recommendation were such that he could have gone almost anywhere. Secondly, he had always known his own story. While he had shared in every tribal tradition since birth, no one had ever tried to indoctrinate him about the politics of being a Native American, and, certainly, no one ever expected John to carry the metaphorical flag. Frankly, he just never struck anyone as that much of an activist.

Lastly, it never occurred to them that he might go to Haskell because, well, he couldn't meet the strict tribal admission requirement regarding one's percentage of

Native American blood...at least as far as anyone had any way of knowing. Each Nation had its own percentage standards, and only registered tribe members were accepted at Haskell. But the moment his determination became clear, inquiries were made, people who knew people talked to other people, and documentation paperwork began showing up in the Ghostwalker file that had never needed to be there before. With generous spirits, but more than a few nervous winks and nods, the General Council officially registered John as a member of the Miccosukee Tribe. John had always suspected that his birth certificate, so ingeniously "aged," probably wouldn't stand up to FBI scrutiny, but when it came to the Bureau of Indian Affairs, anything was possible. The whole tribe waited anxiously for word back from Haskell regarding John's college application.

For his part, John Ghostwalker had always loved his adopted family. He loved everything about it: its history, its sense of community, and its world/life view. Though he was not a joiner, a political animal, nor a touchy-feely kind of guy, the idea of leaving that community cold turkey scared him to his core. But his new-found level of fascination he owed, in part, to his Parkour instructors, Emanuel and Jose Rosario. Their pride in and passion for their Cuban heritage had awakened in John an even greater awareness of the gift he'd been given. In his heart and in his mind, Haskell offered him not only an extension of his own community experience, but a vast expansion of it as well. The central Florida pow wows and Native American art markets he had attended had introduced him to a small portion of the world beyond the Miccosukee and the Seminole, and that diversity was remarkable, but to meet and study with Native Americans from throughout North America was an irresistible draw.

News that mail from Haskell had arrived for John reached the neighborhood four hours before the letter did. The crowd gathered around the letter boxes was unprecedented, and if the mail carrier lingered a bit while John tore open the envelope and scanned the letter, certainly no one faulted her. She had changed her own share of Baby John Doe's diapers.

"Well, what does it say?" Nate asked as Marion and Rachel stood on their tiptoes beside him.

"They let me in!" John said with a grin.

"You've always been one of us, John," said Dan Stone with a loving smile, "but I guess this officially makes you a Native American now too."

"Like *Dances with Wolves*," Rachel quipped, "only different!"

There was a bonfire that night at the elementary school, and a makeshift potluck picnic affair that lasted well into the night. Though its make-up changed constantly throughout the evening, the drum circle was unbroken, and John took more than a few turns himself. Joy is infectious under normal circumstances, certainly, but the open sharing of it that night on the edge of the Everglades was a memory and a story no one there would ever forget.

# Chapter 9: Hot Town

That summer in the city of Miami was filled with excitement and seemingly endless discoveries. John took to Parkour like a baby alligator takes to the swamp, and under the Rosario twins' watchful eyes, his legs and shoulders developed impressive definition, and he earned his instructor's certification by the fourth of July. Free daytime was all about Parkour, a French invention that incorporates many physical disciplines to the purpose of traversing the urban landscape as fast as possible. Obstacles, be they walls, construction sites, or finished buildings, were never to be circumvented if they could be more quickly scaled. To become proficient at Parkour, John needed to hone his gymnastic skills to near Olympic grade perfection. Vaulting was easy for Ghostwalker, but the city pavement is not as forgiving as the mats on the gym floor, so learning how to drop and roll to absorb the shock took more time and attention.

Scaling sheer concrete and/or brick walls was a

constant barometer of his progress. For each new stage of his proficiency, the walls got higher. At first, John needed to jump high enough to plant his elbows on top of a wall before proceeding. Soon, however, if he could jump high enough vertically to catch a two-handed grip, he was good to go...even if it looked a bit ungainly. Eventually, if he could just get one hand, even just his fingertips, up on the wall's lip, he could then swing sideways, catching the top with his other hand and one foot simultaneously. By this time, the fluid grace of the maneuver looked more like ballet then a military obstacle course exercise. The next stage in this progression of capability involved an adjacent wall at a 90 degree angle to the one he wanted to go over. By running full speed at the secondary wall, John sprang up as if he intended to run right up the vertical surface, but, using his leading foot and his forward momentum, he'd push out and upwards toward the primary wall instead. This maneuver, when executed properly, allowed him, in effect, to grab the top of a wall that was closer to twelve or thirteen feet, as opposed to those more like a ten foot high basketball goal. Imagine Dwyane Wade launching himself off Lebron James' thigh, using it as a step ladder on his way to a slam-dunk. He'd easily jump higher than the top of the backboard, and be looking down into the hoop.

While one seldom thinks of trails as a part of the urban landscape, Parkour is all about trails most of us wouldn't recognize if we had a map, but John either learned or invented one nearly every week. His favorite began and ended in the elevated parking structure adjacent to the Metrorail, across the street from Allen Morris Brickell Park. It took him east to Biscayne Bay, out across the short causeway onto Brickell Key, through another expansive parking garage, and up to its roof where the views of the bay and the city were spectacular. Back on the mainland, John turned north along the shoreline and toured both Brickell Park and a section of the Miami River Walk before heading back toward Southeast 1$^{st}$ Avenue and the parking structure where he started.

Closely associated with Parkour, "Free Running" is a very different discipline, a highly competitive one, and more in line with the extreme sports typically seen on ESPN. Rather than getting from point A to point B quickly, Free Running is all about the "wow factor," and the more mid-air twists and summersaults, the better. John had no interest in competition, and the risk factor seemed rather insane to him, but he learned the basic showboating moves anyway, practicing them only during his infrequent night runs. For a young man who preferred to come and go unseen, falling on his ass in broad daylight held no attraction whatsoever.

On a Tuesday morning in August, John set out on his favorite Parkour trail, but stopped short when he noticed that one of the service room doors on the second floor of the parking garage was standing open. Nearby on the floor sat an open toolbox and a five gallon orange bucket which contained several new door locksets, and several corroded ones which had obviously just been replaced. All the new keys were secured together on what looked like an oversized aluminum safety pin. The installer was nowhere to be seen. Without giving himself time to debate the merits, Ghostwalker undid the clasp, palmed one of the keys, and resumed his run. From the very next run, and throughout what was left of the summer, he began each trek with an empty backpack on his shoulders, and he returned with a full one. He was setting up house. His highly erratic routes took in considerably more back alleys, dumpsters, and construction sites. Many thrifty Miamians choose to furnish their new apartments at the gigantic, one-stop-for-anything IKEA furniture store. Others, like John, not so much. He gathered the bulkier junk at night.

# Chapter 10: Property Management

In the days just before John was scheduled to leave for Kansas, he spent a great deal of time with Rachel Blackfeather. To her great delight, he hired her to be his property manager, and explained that he would send her twelve dollars a month if she would (1) keep his workshop bedroom dusted, (2) see to it that the persistent doves did not build any nests up there, and (3) expand his stockpile of "essentials". She wholehearted agreed, without a clue what "essentials" were, or how one might acquire them.

Rachel, always a quick study, soon learned John's recycling route around the neighborhood, and she developed an almost psychic sense of where a new construction site might be discovered. After stern warnings about nails and broken glass, she took to dumpsters and construction scrap piles with all the zeal and efficiency of a swamp rat. Rachel loved the way John found uses for everything, and felt particularly satisfied when she doubled his supply of adhesive products in less than a week.

"Empty" tubes of Liquid Nails, adhesive caulk, and standard silicone caulk, she discovered, were never really empty. John taught her the safe way to cut off the ends of each tube with a razor knife (these were to be cleaned up and saved), how to unroll the cardboard much like her mother did with the dinner roll tubes she bought at Publix, and then how to carefully use a plastic spatula to scrape the remaining product off the inside surface without scratching it. Each adhesive type was stored in marked reseal-able containers like wide-mouth juice bottles, coffee cans with plastic lids, instant coffee, jam, and jelly jars, etc.

When the flattened tube was perfectly clean, Rachel used one of two different plywood "jigs" John had fashioned, and cut away the odd corners. What remained, in essence, was a rectangular-shaped, cardboard backed, mirror. The non-stick aluminum foil inner surface was reflective enough to shave with, and John had one, neatly framed with bronze-like tubing from a discarded headboard, hanging above his tiny recycled RV sink for just that purpose. Rachel realized immediately that John had also used this material for homemade greeting cards. She had received several through the years, but the main reason for the considerable stack he kept flattened under a pile of books had to do with his architectural designs. Whenever Ghostwalker was particularly pleased with one of his original building sketches, he replaced the lead in his mechanical pencil with a carefully modified finishing nail and painstakingly etched the building on the shiny foil surface before framing it and hanging it on his wall or ceiling.

"If it's OK with your folks," John told Rachel while Dan Stone and the Blackfeathers waited with him for the first of several busses that would eventually take him to Lawrence, Kansas, "you can sleep in my room anytime you want."

"Like Higgins on Magnum P.I.," Marion said to her daughter, "you're a majordomo!"

Both Rachel and John stared at her with puzzled looks on their faces, and Marion sheepishly turned to her husband.

"Well, Nathan, I guess I'm showing my age again, aren't I?"

"Yes, dear," Nate said carefully, "but aside from your list of favorite movies, television shows, and rock bands, no one would ever guess."

Marion elbowed him in the ribs as John's bus pulled up. "It's a person who oversees someone else's property when they're away," she explained to her daughter. "It means that you're in charge of John's estate until he comes home."

Moments later, their community ghost child disappeared again.

## Chapter 11: History in the Making

John loved college. He loved being able to choose which classes he'd take, he loved being able (within reason) to choose how many credits he would take each semester, and he loved that, no matter what his class schedule looked like, there were always part-time jobs available on or near the campus. It was the best of all worlds. Although John wasn't big on socializing, at Haskell he still felt very much a part of the tribal family. And, of course, John was delighted to find a space in which he could squat...privately, out of sight, out of mind, and best of all, at no cost whatsoever.

At some point, after the discovery of his room above Nate Blackfeather's workshop, John Ghostwalker learned that his preferred method of making a suitable place for himself in the world was called squatting. What he had previously learned about squatting in gym class, of course, had nothing to do with this new title. He was a squatter. By strict definition, squatters came in two basic varieties:

front door and back door squatters. He was a back door kind of guy; that is, his natural preference was to come and go unseen...even though, heretofore, it had never occurred to him that what he was doing might be considered illegal in most states. Either way, he didn't care much for the terminology and he couldn't wrap his head around why putting unused space to good use was an offense to anyone, but he loved the concept. By and large, Native Americans historically thought of real estate as belonging to everyone, and as long as your use of it was neither destructive, nor an infringement upon someone who got there first, no harm, no foul. Of course when the Europeans showed up and repeatedly took ruthless advantage over the years, land ownership became synonymous with survival. Still, the old way was a deeply cosmic approach to Life, the Universe, and Everything, and it just felt right to John.

He often wondered about the "city apartment" he'd designed in the Brickell parking garage late that summer. There were no personal effects in it yet, but even if there had been, leaving them behind was, well, leaving them behind. If someone stumbled upon it while he was away at school, how could he object? Unused space was unused space. Still, John was quite confident that it would neither be discovered nor missed by anyone. There had been no ceiling, per se, in the ten by twelve foot service closet, and the metal rungs poured into the concrete wall, amidst the electrical, plumbing and fire suppression equipment, went two floors up to nowhere. Perhaps the first draft of the blueprint had indicated a vent or a roof access door, but that detail obviously got lost for good reason. Why climb a ladder two stories to the roof when you could drive your car up there? So when John returned with his purloined key, he saw that there were two black third floor girder beams between the service room's floor and the solid concrete roof 20 feet above. He painted his salvaged plywood's underside black before laying it out across the girders, and thus, his new floor became the service room's new ceiling, and the ladder still appeared to go nowhere and to disappear into blackness. It just got there ten feet sooner, but not so anyone without a flashlight would ever notice. Only by climbing the ladder and putting one's shoulder to the seemingly solid black surface above, could one discover the trap door entrance to John's 120 square foot Brickell loft.

At Haskell Indian Nations University, John took a somewhat different, but no less rewarding, approach. One of the college's oldest buildings had seen many uses since its erection in the 1890's. Although talk of another restoration came up from time to time, funding was far easier to get for new construction. In the meantime, the attic had been given over to the Haskell Cultural Museum staff, and was being used for overflow storage. Fortunately for John, the space had long since been filled, and duly cataloged, but much like the vast government storage facility depicted in the Harrison Ford movie, *Raiders of the Lost Ark*, it had also become largely forgotten. Not having Ghostwalker's penchant for order and design, the various cargo handlers sent there through the years saw no reason to add to their workload by assessing or addressing what their predecessors had done. Instead, they chose a suitable open floor space, deposited their burdens, and moved on. Beginning at the far end of the attic, they had, over the years, built a wall of memories all the way back to the stairs. A few items had even been left, unceremoniously, on the stairway between the second floor and the attic before official word reached the museum officials, who, in turn, commenced their search for more storage space in yet another building.

John knew that messing with items belonging to so many different tribes involved a great deal of spiritual consideration, and even more respect, so he began with a silent and prayerful promise to honor the artifacts strewn around him by giving them both respect and order. It took John less than six hours to compile, compact, and redistribute the historical treasures in such a way as to clear the stairway completely and create a series of narrow maze-like access paths throughout the trove. Should anyone ever need to find something on the room's inventory list, it would now take minutes rather than hours. With the exception, of course, of those items he would be borrowing ... with great reverence and thanksgiving. In the process, the entire contents of the attic had, on average, moved ten feet toward the stairs, and behind this floor-to-roof joists wall of wonders was the college's largest and most exquisitely furnished dorm room. There were three windows (one with its own fire escape), each set off with traditional hand woven tapestry drapes. The furniture was early western eclectic, and the flooring was authentic plush buffalo hide shag. The sweeping and dusting took longer than he might have hoped, but all-in-all, John was very pleased with his new home. As he drifted off to sleep, he wondered whether there was such a thing as a fire escape squatter.

## Chapter 12: Three Degrees of Separation

The next seven years flew by for John Ghostwalker. He packed every possible credit into each semester, year-round, and the more focused his curriculum became, the more he liked it. Because of the relationship between Haskell and the University of Kansas, the transition was seamless, and he received his undergraduate design degree from KU in three years instead of the normal four or five taken by the average Haskell student. He never went home, but rather kept up on the news by exchanging regular email and monthly postal letters with Rachel Blackfeather and Dan Stone. Dan and the Blackfeathers had planned on coming for his graduation until John informed them that he wouldn't be there. He was already enrolled at Georgia Tech for the summer semester, and was having his diploma sent to their house.

His Master's degree program was the best. Not only was every class about architectural design, but he got paid to teach undergraduate classes. He was fully immersed in what was, to him, the most fascinating subject on earth. Most of the creatures on the planet expend some time and energy designing the space in which they live and work, and a few, like bees and ants, create elaborately functional spaces that inspire awe, but only humans have deliberately taken their creation of space far beyond function into the realm of art. John recognized, early on, that a building could tell a story at the same time as it fulfilled its primary purpose. Like prose, poetry and song, architecture could speak to the human heart.

As to matters of the heart, there were more than a few young coeds along the way who took notice of John Ghostwalker. And unlike poor Becky Deacon, most college girls are far more experienced, and far more adept at getting what they want. The most provocative of them were, by and large, nothing less than master puppeteers when it came to the college aged male. The game was easy, the outcome assured, and the egos were large. Like most matters having to do with social interaction, John liked to observe, analyze, and decide. He had a built-in radar system that sensed ulterior motive and an absolute revulsion towards those who would toy with others just for kicks; so, in the face of being utterly shot down--some for the very first time in their lives--several Georgia Tech ladies decided, amongst themselves, that John had to be gay. There was, of course, no other acceptable explanation.

But as easy as it was for Ghostwalker to ignore the cheerleaders, the sorority starlets, and the party girls, there were more than a few of his fellow graduate assistants whom he found decidedly distracting. He was not used to being distracted. It made him feel exposed and vulnerable. Being distracted could slow down, if not destroy, his matriculation time table and delay his return to Miami-Dade county. As much as he enjoyed college, it was only a means to an end, and he wanted the end to come sooner rather than later. He wanted to go home. When he felt himself weakening, he had but to imagine inviting one of the design school coeds back to his living quarters in the basement of the school's main facility support and maintenance building. He had been spoiled at Haskell, and he imagined that most college ladies would find that eclectic room wildly preferable to the damp and noisy basement storage room at Georgia Tech. Anyway, if he stayed focused, he'd be done in less than a year. And whether they accepted his application at FIU or not, he was going back to Florida.

Florida International University took one look at John's application and welcomed him into their PhD program with open arms. His advisor, however, felt constrained to comment on his file at their first meeting.

"Mr. Ghostwalker," she said, looking at him over the top of his records folder, "I'm Dr. Franklin. Welcome. I must admit that I have never heard of anyone obtaining these two degrees in this short a period of time. Two possible explanations come to mind. Either the standards at three respected schools have simultaneously collapsed overnight, or you are the most gifted and compulsively obsessed student I've ever met. That, of course, begs the question as to whether there are emotional and/or mental health issues here that I need to be concerned about. Tell me about your social life, John."

He was stunned. He might just as well have been thrust suddenly out onto a stage where a blinding spotlight focused, relentlessly, down upon him. Nothing in his academic career had prepared him for a question like that, and he suddenly felt like his life was on trial. It must have shown on his face.

"I mean no offence, Mr. Ghostwalker," she said with a smile, "and I am not judging you, really, but I am concerned that you might have unrealistic expectations about earning a PhD here at FIU. I'm a firm believer in balance, and for the past four and a half years, anyway, it appears that you have exhibited little or none of it in your life. So, let me come at it another way. You've obviously driven hard and fast to get here. Why?"

As John thought about what his new advisor had said, he relaxed in his chair, and felt the heat of the imaginary spotlight disappear. He laughed gently at himself as he met Dr. Franklin's gaze.

"The truth is, Dr. Franklin, I just wanted to come home. I used to tell myself that school was the only thing in the way of my getting to design a real building, so I wanted to get it over with as fast as possible. But I got home the night before last, and then my whole family, well, my whole neighborhood really, threw a picnic party for me yesterday. That's when I realized how homesick I really was. As far as the social thing goes, the Miccosukee tribe was my only social network until I fell in love with Brickell, and discovered Parkour. I got my Parkour instructor's certificate just before leaving for Haskell, but you're right, I never even made much time for that while I was away. But I'm back now. I'm home. In fact, my favorite running trail took me right past, well, actually right *over* this building, and I set my sights on coming here way back then. Don't send me to the Chattahoochee funny farm quite yet, OK?"

"Well, Mr. Ghostwalker," Dr. Franklin said with a damp sparkle in her eyes, "there's more to you than meets the permanent record! No, I guess I won't call the shrink and have you hauled away yet, but I will be watching you. Let's get to work."

– The Ghostwalker File –

## Chapter 13: The Doctor Will See You Now

The significance of the beautiful walnut cane with the big red gift bow on it was lost on him momentarily. The Sunday picnic at the elementary school was decorated in celebration of yet another graduation he had decided not to attend. Even "Iko, Iko," playing in the background on Rachel's boom box went right over his head. It was only when he read the carefully carved inscription on the cane that he burst out laughing with everybody else. "To: Dr. John. Congratulations from your very proud Miccosukee family."

Three years at FIU was a bit more time and commitment than he had hoped for, but Dr. Franklin had been correct. The stakes were much higher, and the levels of expectation were, at times, overwhelming. His dissertation, *Urban Architecture and the Reacquisition of Non-Visible Space,* had brought John far more attention than he liked having to deal with, but it had also revitalized a long-standing discussion in the field: Does art in architecture need to be wasteful? He was heavily recruited during his final year, and much sought after as a speaker when his dissertation was published and reviewed. As much as he shied away from crowds in general, addressing a group of students and/or educators about architectural design was extremely satisfying. To be paid for it seemed almost wrong. On his first day at Jacobs & Associates, he was invited to join the design team for the "Brickell Town Towers," their newest multi-use high rise project, and he was urged to return a phone call from Los Angeles. Frank Ghary wanted to consult with *him* about Miami Beach's newly opened New World Center. The surreal nature of that experience left him breathless.

"Dr. Ghostwalker," said the distinguished voice, "thank you for returning my call. Dr. Alfred Andrews, at FIU, insisted that I read your dissertation, and I'm glad he did. I've had some after thoughts about the Miami Beach project, particularly the performance space, and I wondered if you'd consider a preliminary consult?"

It went on like that for several weeks. John might have been tempted to run off into the Everglades and hide out with Dan Stone, except Dan had rented an efficiency apartment near the casino and returned his island to its natural state. Spending Saturday nights in his old room over Nate's shop helped a lot, and there was something very comforting about his "apartment" at the Brickell parking garage that kept him grounded. There were just too many changes all at once. While he was in school, he'd always had a student mail box, an address. In the real world, unless he wanted to commute to the Blackfeather's, he had to get a post office box. His first paycheck at Jacobs & Associates was staggering. While other associates grumbled about being "slave labor," John felt suddenly rich. But when he learned what the average young professional paid for rent, car payments, gas, and auto insurance in Miami, he began to understand. The list of "grownup" changes he was forced to make began with the purchase of a cell phone with a calling plan, and the logical conclusion would seem to be purchasing a car and renting a real apartment, but these last, he simply could not bring himself to do.

His head was still spinning when the tribe threw him a picnic party to celebrate his achievements, and so he was not prepared for the red haired women who seemed to show up in his life out of nowhere.

"John, this is my new friend, Mac," Rachel said, a hot dog in one hand and a stranger in the other. "Mac, this is my big brother, John."

"Glad to meet you, John," the redhead said, letting go of Rachel's hand and reaching out to him.

"Same here," he said, but barely. He took her hand, but nothing else seemed willing to come out of his mouth.

"Congratulations on your degree and your new job," Mac said. "People here are very proud of you."

Rachel scrunched up her brow and took back Mac's hand, just to stop John from shaking it off of her wrist. "We were just going over to the swings. Come with."

John followed obediently, carrying his new cane absently in his left hand, struggling to reconnect his brain to his tongue.

"I told Mac all about you," Rachel said proudly. "Mac moved into the old Decker place a few months ago. She's really fixing it up nice."

They arrived at the playground, and Rachel was careful to select a swing that left John and Mac side-by-side. John set his cane gently against the silver swing posts and settled down into the canvas seat, where his knees came almost to his chin. Mac had assumed a cross-legged yoga-like position, and was already swinging.

"Rachel tells me you're a Parkour instructor," Mac said as she went by. "I've always wanted to try that."

"I'm years out of shape," John managed.

"Good," Mac said, "then maybe I won't feel quite so wimpy at first! Where do I sign up?"

The following week seemed to drag at a snail's pace. John dutifully toured the New World Center complex, accessing anything he might consider space that could be reclaimed without disrupting the amazing look, feel, and acoustics of the somehow grand, yet intimate, symphony hall. His boss, Abraham Jacobs, was beside himself at the prospect that his firm, having been overlooked for the high profile home town project, might get a chance to improve upon the work of an international grandmaster like Ghary. Despite his considerable resume, none of Jacob's buildings had ever even made the short list for the Pritzker Architecture Prize, let alone won it like Frank Ghary. Just being brought in for a consult was a feather he would wear proudly in his cap...even though it was only because of the new associate he'd just hired.

John felt the pressure, but even with his mind wandering often to the coming weekend and his first Parkour student, several ideas leapt out at him as he was guided through the symphony hall by a staffer. From the majesty of the high, wonderfully sculpted, walls and ceilings of the performance space, to the grandness of the campus complex throughout, it struck him as having reached only a fraction of Director Michael Thompson's vision for the New World Symphony project. This block-sized campus in the heart of Miami Beach, had become the go-to place for the best of the very best from every top music school and conservatory in the world. The "satellite" nature of the class and practice rooms certainly enhanced the educational capabilities of the program by leaps and bounds, but Frank Ghary's telephone suggestion that more could be done with the main performance hall was true. There was usable space within the amazing concert hall Ghary had created, and John looked forward to pointing it out more specifically.

The "Brickell Town Towers" project was in its final stages of construction, and the principles were hoping to begin Stage I occupancy shortly, so John's responsibilities on the final review team were far less stressful. Aside from scoping out an incredible squat apartment for himself, maybe even one with an ocean view, there wasn't much for him to focus on there. The bulk of his responsibilities lay in the area of fact and spec checking, and that he could nearly do in his sleep.

No, the big item on his agenda was getting ready for his new student. He couldn't put his finger on why Mac had captivated him so easily, but there was no denying that she had.

## Chapter 14: Panoramic Views

    Like all novice Parkour classes, Mac's began in the gym. She wasn't as strong as she would need to be, but that would come. What impressed John most was her coordination and flexibility. She picked up the rolling fall much faster than he had, and seemed able to return gracefully to her feet from any position.
    "Yoga," she said when he paid her a compliment. "Tried classes, but couldn't get into the scene, so I study on my own."
    "It works for you," John said, "but we've got to strengthen your upper body. I don't think the running's going to be a problem. Let's try the horse next."
    Throughout the two hour class, John was impressed by Mac's ability to communicate simply and efficiently. No jibber-jabber. She usually comprehended instantly, but if she had a question, it was succinct and to the point. They learned things about each other naturally and utterly without drama. Without ever trying, Mac exhibited a great

intelligence, but with no need to show it off. She was like no other woman he had ever met...save perhaps several of the octogenarian Miccosukee women who had grandmothered him through the years. They too convinced him that what you thought you saw was nothing compared to the essence of womanhood lying just out of sight beneath the surface. Mac was definitely an old soul.

He had assumed (hopefully) that Mac's interest in Parkour was a "move", and for the first time in his life, he didn't mind. But after the two gym-based classes, he was forced to check his ego and reassess. They got on famously, and with a tang of chagrin, John decided that friendship with Mac was well worth the thumping it would cost his ego. Their first run was like the ones the Rosario twins had taken him on. The walls were low, the drops were safe, and the views were spectacular. Her breathless appreciation of the Miami skyline and Biscayne Bay was gratifying on several levels.

"My god!" she said as they topped the parking garage on Brickell Key. "This town looks even better in person than it does on CSI Miami!"

"I haven't grown tired of it yet," John said. "Let's head back."

They were his least favorite words, but he said them twice a week with all the dignity and grace he could muster.

John's notes and sketches for Frank Ghary and Maestro Thompson had to get past Abraham Jacobs first, so when he was summoned to the boss' office, he was prepared for the worst. The only instructions Abraham had given him were all too simple: "Nothing crazy." From his first sketch, he knew he had exceeded those boundaries considerably, but that could not be helped. It was what it was. There were two strangers in Jacob's office, and without introductions, his boss pointed him to a lone seat at the far end of the desk/conference table.

"You're insane," Jacob's said without preamble, "just fucking insane. You know that, don't you?"

The strangers were suppressing smiles.

"Dr. Franklin suggested as much on my first day at FIU," John replied, "but nothing's been legally confirmed in writing."

"Well this might nail down that little detail," his boss said, rising from his chair. "We've got witnesses this time."

He introduced Angelo Rodriquez and Hector Soyos as the owners of Coral Gables Construction. "I just wanted to confirm how crazy you were, but these guys may be crazier. They say it might be do-able, and have agreed to help us put together a full blown proposal. Perhaps we'll all be certifiable before this is over, young Ghostwalker, but it's going to be a hell of a ride!"

For the next hour, while both architects sketched furiously, the four of them brainstormed John's various ideas for the "Maestro's Sky Mall." The greatest challenges came from the builders, but always because the materials necessary to make the project safe were typically not hung out in front of God and everybody.

"Remember the Kansas City Hyatt disaster?" Angelo Rodriquez asked John. "It happened before you were born, but I'll bet you studied it more than once while you were at school. We need the kind of cable washers those builders were *supposed* to use, but didn't. And you don't want anyone to see them?"

"Exactly," John replied. He had, in fact, studied the 1981 collapse of the walkways suspended above the Kansas City Hyatt hotel's lobby. The architect's plans, not to mention code and common sense, called for square steel washers in excess of three feet across as the cable-mounted base for the poured concrete walkways, but to save approximately $400 apiece, the builder had substituted a much smaller round washer. One hundred and fourteen people lost their lives, over 200 were seriously injured, and the lawsuits dragged on for years. "That's the easy part. What I can't figure out, is how to allow folks to see through them!"

"Well, good luck with that!" his boss laughed, turning back to the builders. "John's right though, it's really all about smoke and mirrors; well, actually, angles and mirrors. By the way, Ghostwalker, using Ghary's New York windows concept was a nice touch. He's got to love that!"

It is simply called "New York by Ghary," and while planted quite solidly on Spruce Street in Manhattan, the 870 foot stainless steel and glass high rise seems to ungulate against the skyline. It may be the tallest residential structure in the Western Hemisphere, and while one might easily imagine that its inspiration came solely from the future, Frank Ghary credits the bay window. Instead of celebrating the spectacular city views through the two dimensional plate glass window, Ghary wrapped each window around the tenants on three sides. Inside and out, the simple concept was nothing less than stunning.

"We're upping the ante some with two more dimensions," John quipped, "but it's the perfect opportunity."

"And the big breathing holes?" Angelo asked. "You really want those?"

"They're not for breathing air," John said. "They're for air being propelled by sound. It's a music space. No free flow of air, no free flow of music."

As the developing sectional sketches spread across the conference table, the sky walk came to life. Beginning and ending with modifications to the existing elevators at the left and right rear of the concert hall's performance space, the plexi-glass trail wandered its serpentine way through space, twenty feet above the audience and the stage. There were small see-through offices, individual rehearsal rooms, a tiny café with a half-dozen tables, and even a "wooded park". Bulbous potted ferns and tiny trees would appear suspended in mid air. One see-through room, just off the walkway's midway point, would, if John had his way, actually be capable of being lowered to stage level and back. His sketched likeness of Yo-Yo Ma performing on his cello wasn't going to help law enforcement personnel identify the great artist, but the effect on everyone in Jacob's office was electric.

"Probably wouldn't want to play up there in a dress," Hector laughed. "Bad enough, spotlights in your face, but having them up your skirt is another thing altogether!"

"Glare," John said as he studied the rectangular plexiglass sections. "There's always going to be some wicked glare issues somewhere, depending on the lighting. We need to consider that."

"Ever have a gerbil?" Abraham Jacobs asked with a chuckle. "My kids loved them."

"Of course!" John said, and they both began rounding off the square edges with their pencils. Bay windows became bubbles, adding considerably to the feeling of being suspended in mid-air and surrounded by view.

"It's come to this," Hector said to his partner. "We've sunk to building hamster habitats!"

"Maybe we can work our way up to McDonald's playgrounds," Angelo replied with a grin.

Abraham punched the button on his intercom as John tossed down the last sketch. "Get me that video animator guy we used on the Pinkerton thing," he said to Mandy Hawkins at the front desk. "I think his name was Daboul...Rick, maybe."

"Yes sir," said the disembodied voice as the four of them stepped back from the table and stared in silence.

## Chapter 15: BFF

It dawned on John quite suddenly, the reality that he had never knowingly made a friend in his life. Not one. So the idea that Mac was his best friend seemed cheapened somehow. Then he remembered the Rosario twins, and Dan Stone, and sort of thought that they must be friends too. He didn't necessarily dislike people in general, and he was certainly extremely fond of a great many people, but being friendly and having friends are two very different things. He had always had what he thought family should be, but his feelings for Mac were not like that. He couldn't wait to see her again. He loved spending time with her. They shared runs, meals, and as of late, even movies and live music events, all with an ease and an affability that perpetually created feelings of joyousness. John felt increasingly ignorant in the face of this unfamiliar terrain, and often wished that he had another friend, like Mac, to whom he could address the question that hounded him around the clock: If these extremely powerful feelings weren't love, then what were they?

Mac often met him for lunch, attended company affairs with him, picnicked with John and his Miccosukee family on Sunday afternoons, but when asked innocent questions like "How long have you guys been dating?" they both laughed and said that it "wasn't like that." But it was like that, well without the intimacy, but even on that front, it was hard for John to imagine feeling more intimately involved with anyone. Semantics had always been easy for him; words meant something, or they didn't. But that was his rational, intellectual self at its best. Nothing he had learned about Life, the Universe, and Everything to date was in the least bit helpful to him when it came to his feelings about Mac. Even the depth of his ignorance was apparently lost on him.

"What did you say your friend Mac's last name was?" his boss asked him one morning after a company dinner event the night before. "She's a remarkable young lady."

John stood frozen in place, but the world seemed to spin around him and he reached out and grabbed the office door post for support. "I never asked," he said quietly. "I probably ought to do that, huh boss?"

"Might be nice," Abraham said with a chuckle. "You are a strange one, Mr. Ghostwalker, a strange one indeed."

That night, over dinner at Carraba's in South Beach, John tried to ask several times. Afterwards, they walked along the Boardwalk under a nearly full moon, and he still couldn't think of a way to bring it up. It was as if some inner warning poster threatened dire penalties should he broach that subject. The cab ride back to Mac's Mini Cooper in the Brickell parking garage was different somehow, a little tense certainly, but it wasn't until she drove away that the house of ignorance cards fell into jumbled piles around his feet. They were both doing it. It wasn't just him. Mac had been meeting John on the corner across the street, or here in this parking garage, for months now, and she had never once asked him where he lived, or about which car in the sometimes empty garage was his.

He had barely climbed up into his loft when someone knocked on the steel door down in the service room below. No one had ever knocked on that door before. Never having surprise visits and/or "walk-ins" was the core motivation of a back door squatter. Sure, maintenance people occasionally came and went down there without ever being aware of his presence, but no one ever knocked. John flipped on the wall mounted computer monitor he had salvaged from a dumpster, and cycled through the building's eight security camera views until he came to the one which used to show his door. He worked a computer mouse until the remote controlled camera returned to the position in which he'd originally found it. There stood Mac, in lo-res black and white, looking directly up at the camera.

When he opened the door, she walked past him, glanced around, and then ascended the ladder. After stepping into his loft, Mac poked her head back into the hatch opening and called down to him. "I realize that this might seem awkwardly weird, but we need to talk."

John turned off the service room light and headed up the ladder. If he was ever asked to explain this behavior, he would reference Charles Grodin's response to a similar query by Diane Cannon in *Heaven Can Wait*: "Her will was too strong."

Mac was sitting on his drafting stool, the only chair in the room, so John pulled at the edge of the hammock he had created from a well-worn jib sail he'd recovered from a trash pile behind the Brickell Sail Loft, and he settled in to face her. Mac fished briefly in her backpack, retrieved an old cigar box, and placed it in his hands.

"My name is Sean McKnight," she said. "I don't have many friends, but the ones I do have call me Mac. I'm a freelance headhunter, and I'm a squatter too...but a front door squatter actually. You popped up all over the net, and on the surface, you were a headhunter's dream. But you were also a lot like me, so instead of trying to find you a job, I started researching you for my collection. It's a hobby," she said, indicating with her hand that he should open the cigar box.

John flipped off the rubber band and opened the lid. Inside he saw thirteen thumb drives of various brands and colors, each marked with a number.

"Subjects one through twelve were a blast. I love studying interesting people, especially from a safe distance, and there never seemed to be any harm in it. But then you came along and turned me into a stalker. I admit it," Mac said, throwing out her hands as if in surrender to her fate, "I just couldn't stop, so I moved to the Everglades, of all places, to your neighborhood, just to fill in the details I couldn't find on the web."

Mac was really cooking right along, and though John opened and closed his mouth slowly, like a fish out of water, he was either unable or unwilling to interrupt her.

"It might have all ended right there. I'm not good at networking, and I just couldn't bring myself to go around knocking on Miccosukee front doors, but then Rachel just walked up, introduced herself to me, and welcomed me to the neighborhood!" She seemed to come out of rant mode for a second and looked more squarely into John's eyes. "My god! Aren't they incredible? All of them!"

He might have agreed, but Mac never gave him a chance, shifting instead, right back into high gear.

"Anyway," she said breathlessly, "They love you and they love bragging on you, and I don't know what I thought was going to happen. I mean I knew I'd have to tell you at some point, or not, who knows? But I never meant to fall in love with you, and I never meant to creep you out, and you're the best friend I ever had."

She was down the ladder and opening the door before John managed to extract himself from the hammock, set down the cigar box, and start down after her.

"Say goodbye to Rachel for me," she said with a wave as the Mini Cooper pulled away. "I'm really sorry, John."

## Chapter 16: The Man in the Mirror

John was sorry too. Of all the times not to have a vehicle. He looked frantically around the empty parking garage, as if his wounded partner, having seen the bad guys escape, would roar up the ramp in their battered patrol car, throw open the passenger door, and shout: "Get in!" Upon reflection, however, aside from the movie-like melodrama, a car chase in Miami traffic—no matter how romantic—wasn't likely to turn out well. And in the end, John just wasn't that guy. But who was he?

He had to admit that thumb drives one through twelve were pretty fascinating, in a weird-by-association kind of way, but knowing that number thirteen was about him kept John from dawdling. When he finally plugged it into his laptop, he wondered how anything that might be on it could possibly explain Sean "Mac" McKnight. He discovered, however, that the sheer magnitude and depth of Mac's research--from the web stuff, to the probing interviews with half the Miccosukee tribe, to the notes on the time they spent together--said a lot about the mysterious redhead...primarily, that she was easily his match when it came to having an obsessive-compulsive side, and a vicarious approach to socialization. Beyond that, he tried not to think about what Dr. Franklin might have to say on the subject.

All he kept thinking was: "She loves me. What can be so wrong with that?"

To which he always replied: "Then why did she run away?" and "Should I be afraid?"

The route to both answers led him home to the Everglades, so in the morning he called a cab and had it drop him off at the old Decker place. The Mini Cooper was not in the driveway, so he settled in on the stoop to consider his options. Word got around fast that Dr. Ghost was sitting on the steps, right out there in front of God and everybody, so it wasn't long before Rachel Blackfeather walked up and settled down beside him. John was, once again, forced to consider his ability to randomly disassociate from the everyday realities of Life, the Universe, and Everything.

"Rachel," he said, "whatever has happened to you?"

"What do you mean?"

"A couple days ago, you were a cute, scrawny kid. Now, just look at you! You're beautiful!"

"Well, thank you, big brother," she said as her cheeks turned red. "You've been away a lot."

"Literally and figuratively," he agreed. "I sometimes miss the stuff that's right under my nose, don't I?"

"Duh!" Rachel said. "You have noticed that Mac really likes you, I hope?"

"Well, perhaps I've been a little slow on the uptake, but that's why I'm here. She is pretty amazing, isn't she?"

"Just like you."

"Hmm."

They sat in silence for a while. Then John turned to Rachel and said, "Did she ever mention where she moved here from?"

"No."

"Did she ever say anything about family, friends, any addresses come up?"

"No, John. Why?"

"What about her last name, Rach, did she ever mention that to you?"

"Well, no, I don't think so. What's all this about?"

"McKnight, Sean McKnight is her name. She said to tell you goodbye, Rachel, so there's a good chance that she's already gone."

"Gone where?" Rachel asked as she rose and tried the front door. It was locked, so she grabbed the magnetic key box which was stuck to the back side of the boot scrape just off the walk near the bottom of the steps. "What did you do?"

"I don't know," John said. "I just don't know."

"Did you ever see this place before the Deckers moved away?" Rachel said as they toured the empty house.

"No."

"It was a dump. Mac cleaned, fixed the drywall, painted, everything. It's like new in here."

"She's a squatter like me," John said, "only she doesn't sneak in and out like I do. She lives there right out in the open, and, according to her own ethical compass, she pays rent by doing home improvement work."

"But the owners know, right?"

"Nope. They're gone, or dead, or who knows? Mac researches vacant places, and if it looks like nobody's minding the store, she just moves in and makes herself at home."

"So she could be anywhere?" Rachel asked.

"I'm afraid so. She could be anywhere."

"But you're going to try and find her, aren't you, John?"

"Oh yes. I'm going to try very hard to find her," John sighed, "but first I'm going to tell you a story about why she moved in here in the first place."

He retrieved his laptop from his backpack, discovered

there was no Wi-Fi signal, and got to his feet. "To the bat cave, Robin," he said as he headed out across the neighborhood.

Once they settled into his old room above her dad's shop, Rachel sprawled out in the fishing net hammock, and John in the recycled wheelchair/recliner, the internet came to life and he Googled "Sean McKnight." In a somewhat chilling nod to Frank Herbert, Mac's website was called "Hunter-Seeker.com," and the logo was a horizontal, free floating office vacuum mail cylinder with "Hunter-Seeker, LLC" emblazoned on the side. As he read the home page info, the somewhat transparent logo slowly and deliberately crisscrossed the screen in a systematic grid-search pattern, leaving no pixel unsearched. At the bottom of the page, in quotations and italicized script, was Mac's PR mission statement: "*If the employees you need are out there, I'll find them.*" John spun the laptop around and handed it to Rachel.

"So you found her!" Rachel said after scanning the page. "That's good, right?"

"I can call, text, and/or email her, yes, but you won't find a physical address there."

"Well, did you do any of those yet?"

"Not yet. Let me tell you the story." He handed Rachel the old cigar box. "That's her job," he said, pointing to the computer, "and this is her hobby."

He spoke while Rachel scanned the thumb drives in numerical order. When he was finished with his tale, John smiled at the incredulous look on Rachel's face. She lay staring at one of his shiny etchings on the ceiling above, but the emotional tug-of-war showed plainly in her subtle, but ever-morphing expressions. Into the profound silence came the squeaking of the screen door below them and the sound of Marion's voice.

"You guys OK up there? I made some lunch. Come join me."

"Holy shit, Batman!" Rachel said softly.

"What was that, honey?"

"Nothing, mom. We'll be right over."

## Chapter 17: The Ghost in the Machine

With *carte blanche* office assistance which might have led to a few bruised egos, John finished the preliminary blueprints for the Sky Mall in a couple of days, but when he saw the video and computer presentations Rick Daboul brought in a week later, he was blown away.

"How did he do this?" he asked his beaming boss. "This is real footage of the existing symphony space with our stuff suspended right in there. It's incredible, isn't it?"

"My thoughts, exactly," Abraham said with gusto. "I'm thinking of a whole new ad campaign when this thing gets built: 'How do you improve on perfection?'" he said dramatically, spreading his hands meaningfully across the outside image of the symphony hall on the big flat screen in front of them. He used the mouse to zoom right through the glass wall and into the performance space. "'Just call Jacobs & Associates!'"

"Getting a little ahead of ourselves, aren't we? And why not 'Jacobs, Ghostwalker & Associates' while you're at it?"

"Now who's getting ahead of themselves?" his boss said with a laugh. "Are we ready to send this to Los Angeles?"

"I can't see why not."

He just couldn't call. Maybe it was his inner resentment of cell phones in general. Maybe it was knowing that his rambling voice would be recorded, forever, that put him off. But it was what it was, and after several days of pretending he'd get around to calling Mac, John got real and began to compose an email message instead. (He hated everything about texting.) Three days later, after changing "Dear Mac" to "Hey Mac!" and then to "Hello!" several times around on the draft, John just hung there on his dilemma like an exhausted hamster, prostrate on its plastic wheel. He was getting nowhere, and if thumb drive number thirteen had taught him nothing else, it had revealed, beyond all debate, the magnitude of his romantic ineptitude. It's not like he was burned so badly his first time out of the chute that the emotional scars left him traumatized; he'd never been persuaded into the chute in the first place, let alone burst wildly out of the opposite gate. He was, as Abraham Jacobs might have said, *verklempt*.

Bobby, the anal-compulsively reliable security guard, passed across the rotating garage views on his wall monitor, reminding John that he had never returned the nearest camera in his area to its alternate stance, and as he did so, a ray of hope flashed in the more logical hemisphere of his brain. He reached underneath the hinged drafting table which was secured to his wall with Tap-con screws, and patted the old Dell PC tower affectionately.

"I saved you from the landfill, Dell," he told it earnestly, "now it's your turn to save me."

The ancient PC had no working DVD/CD drive (John used the CD tray as a cup holder), ran a hopelessly outdated version of the Windows operating system, and was physically held together primarily with duct tape. Like Nate had often told him: "If you can't fix it with duct tape, you shouldn't oughta own it." Dell was like a roommate, and had John kept track of how many one-sided conversations he had had with the beat up old machine, he might have found it easier to worry less about the possible motes in Sean McKnight's psychological eye. As it was, he was only thinking about Dell's hard drive brain right then.

He worked the mouse, opened folders, and selected a file by double clicking on it. The grainy black and white video image was the same as it might have been on any day, except for one significant detail. The rear end of a two-tone Mini-Cooper sat squarely in the fish-eyed picture. After exporting the video file to a thumb drive, John went to work on his laptop. PhotoShop would have been nice, but the watered-down tools in his version of PrintShop would have to do. He captured the image he wanted from the paused video, converted it to a .jpeg file, and went to work on cleaning it up. Almost immediately his handiwork confirmed what he thought he already remembered. The car had Florida plates. The numbers came into readable focus soon thereafter, and by the time he was done magnifying and tweaking, he was reasonably certain it was a Monroe County plate.

Whatever was going to happen, or not happen, between himself and Mac was surely going to happen, or not happen, in person...he hoped. John went back to work that morning with a renewed sense of purpose and direction. As it happened, he was scheduled to take his weekly turn on oversight watch at the Brickell Town Towers, his favorite associate obligation. He understood why the others hated it, but he pitied them for it whenever the inevitable whining began again. Still, to their everlasting befuddlement, he voluntarily covered their turns for them whenever he could.

"The air conditioning in that trailer office sucks."

"A folding chair, two saw horses, and a piece of filthy plywood are no excuse for a work space."

"The dust, it never lets up. It's taken years off my life, I just know it."

"Those guys don't look, they leer."

Well, that one, maybe, but for the most part, it was a joy for John to be out of the office, the sea breeze was revitalizing, the "work space" allotted to the Jacobs' associates had a spectacular view of Biscayne Bay, and the construction workers were real human beings who took pride in what they did. Most of them spoke Spanish amongst themselves, but always switched to English whenever he walked up. Something about them, as a group, reminded him of the Miccosukee tribe, an unspoken bond that resonated with humanity. They took to him immediately, most likely because he behaved exactly as he had been raised to behave. If someone was struggling with a heavy load, you pitched in without thinking about it. If a worker needed an extra hand, you offered two without asking permission. If someone was falling behind, you stopped what you were doing until you'd helped them catch up. His "office casual" clothes took some abuse, but he liked being one of the guys, and soon no one gave his coming and going, or his borrowing of their tools, a second thought.

Because of this, his bay view apartment was coming along nicely. Had his tweaking of the blueprints negatively impacted anything or anyone, he might have had a twinge of guilt, but as it was, it was the most beautiful "wasted space" he had ever seen. In his mind, it rivaled the symphony hall project, and he couldn't wait to move in. If his meddling had cost the builder anything in time and/or materials, he knew he had more than paid for it in both sweat equity and blueprint modification. Waste is costly business. The ability to fashion one's living space as it was being constructed was as exhilarating as it was inspiring. The inspiring thing was still fuzzy, but somehow there was a bigger picture forming. He just had to wait for it to reveal itself.

## Chapter 18: In for a Penny

Billy Stillwater was the youngest cop on the Miccosukee Reservation police force. He enrolled in the police academy right out of high school, and was hired by the tribe upon his graduation with one proviso which he had joyously accepted. He committed to taking at least one college course every semester until he received a degree in the subject of his own choosing. And, as long as he performed his duties with honor, and got passing grades, his education would cost him nothing. Better even than that, Marion had whispered to John, that Billy was rumored to be interested in Rachel.

John asked Marion to invite Billy to the Sunday picnic. "Just tell him I'd like to chat with him for a few minutes."

Marion nodded, and smiled knowingly, thinking that Rachel was really behind the request. John made no effort to correct her. On Sunday, while carrying a crock pot over to the elementary school for Marion, John got a grilling from his not-so-little sister.

"Nothing? You didn't even leave a message, write an email, anything?"

"No."

"Why? What are you going to do?"

"Talk to Billy Stillwater. Look, here he comes."

"Oh my god!" Rachel said with exasperation. "You're as bad as mom. I'm leaving."

"But I thought you were the detective? You just want me to find Mac by myself, is that it?"

That stalled her just long enough.

"Hello Rachel," Billy said. "What's up Ghostman? Marion said you wanted to see me."

As he set the crock pot on the table and extended his hand to Billy, John did a quick read of Rachel's face. In less than a heartbeat's time, she went from being angry at what she assumed was a set-up, to being miffed that Billy's full attention had turned so quickly to her brother.

"Yes, Billy. Thanks. I need some help finding someone, and all I've got is a Monroe County license plate number. Could you run it for me by any chance?"

"I heard that Mac left in a hurry," he said. "I'm sorry about that, but running her plate would cost me my job for sure...unless there's a good reason to believe that she's broken the law and is fleeing prosecution?" he added with one raised eyebrow.

"No," John said a bit too quickly, "it's nothing like that."

"There must be something you can do to help us," Rachel burst in.

John couldn't have scripted it better if he'd had the opportunity. Billy Stillwater straightened up as if he were suddenly wearing his uniform instead of his blue jeans, squared his shoulders, and gave his full attention to Rachel.

"Well, Rachel," Billy said thoughtfully, "there may be one thing I can do to point you in the right direction."

After they ate and made the minimal social rounds, Billy drove John and Rachel down to the police station. "Hey, Tubby! Sorry, I mean Sergeant, is it OK if I show John and Rachel our new toy?"

"You keep playing with that thing and you're gonna break it," the desk Sergeant laughed, "but sure, nothing's going on right now. Hello Miss Rachel, Dr. John, how are you guys?"

"Good, Tubby," Rachel said as John stuck his hand up over the desk. "You?"

"I'm good too, thanks." Tubby said, taking John's hand and shaking it hard. "Sorry about Mac, John."

"Word travels fast," John laughed.

"Like the wind on the moccasin trail," Tubby said with a shrug of his beefy shoulders.

Billy led them into the empty squad room where the department insignia screen saver was emblazoned on a 52" wall monitor and he wiggled the mouse on the desk nearby. The computer desktop appeared on the screen, and Billy double-clicked on an icon called "T.I.P."

"It's called a Traffic Information Program, and every county's got their own. Technically, we're only supposed to see the Reservation cams, but nobody ever broke the program down that far."

While they watched, Billy brought up a menu and began filling in data about Mac's Mini-Cooper. When he finished, he turned to John. "When do you think she split?"

"Week ago, Wednesday, I think" John said. "Real late on the night before the full moon."

Billy added the date, selected a twelve hour scan, and clicked the "Real Time" button for the southernmost camera in Miami-Dade County. A remarkably clear shot of US 1 near the Florida City Raceway gas station filled the screen, and motorists drove north and south below the camera lens.

"Cool, right?" Billy said, looking at Rachel. "Now watch this."

He clicked on the "Scan" button and they were looking

at a nighttime shot from the same camera, but it was racing in fast forward while a timer in the upper right corner of the screen clocked the digital record's progress. At a little after 1:00 A.M., according to the yellow numerals on the digital counter, the blurring rush of traffic froze, and there in the south bound lane, captured in a red box shaped outline, was the slightly blurred image of a blue and white Mini-Cooper. Billy made a few selections with the mouse, moving the car forward, click by click, and then tightened up the red box until it was just larger than the license plate. With another few clicks, the license plate filled the screen.

"Is that your plate number?" Billy said, like a cocky magician wrapping up a card trick.

"That's it," John said.

"Then Elvis has left the building heading south," Billy said.

"But you really can't look at Monroe County cameras to see where she went?" Rachel asked.

"Not without a signed warrant."

"But at least we narrowed our search down to one of 4,500 islands." John said. "How bad can that be?"

After Billy dropped them off at the Blackfeather's, and Rachel went in to see what her folks were watching on TV, John walked through the back fence gate into Grandmother Renee's small yard. He walked up her back steps and knocked lightly on her screen door. John was never sure to whom, if anyone, Grandmother Renee Persons was actually related, but in this neighborhood, that was superfluous. Here, she was everybody's grandmother.

"Grandmother?" he called through the screen. The TV went instantly mute.

"Come in, child," she answered from the living room. "I've missed you."

"Is something broken?" he quipped as he bent over her

easy chair and kissed her silky grey head.

"Oh, you sassy boy!" she laughed, swatting him away and pointing to the old rocker where he had always loved to sit. "I do not miss you because you fix things for me...but I must admit that my television picture has never looked better!" She chuckled at herself. "What brings you to me? A red-headed woman, perhaps?"

John shook his head in surrender to what he liked to call "the one rule of the tribe:" News not shared is not newsworthy.

"It is our way, child. Even a ghost has few secrets in the tribe. What do you intend to do about this woman friend of yours?"

"That's the question, Grandmother. If a woman runs away, is it because she wishes to be left alone, or because she wants to be followed?"

"Most of the time, I'm sure she does not know herself, and her answer might change from one day to the next, from one moment to the next, so how could you be expected to know? That is her wind."

"Right!" John said with relief. "How the hell should I know anything about her wind?" John rocked in the silence for several bewildering seconds before looking back at the old woman. "What exactly is her wind, Grandmother?"

"It is the force that moves her forward on her journey of renewal."

"Right. And I have no way of knowing what's going on with someone else's wind?"

"Of course not, child."

"So how do I know whether I'm supposed to try and find her?"

"That is your wind."

"Of course it is." John rose, kissed her head fondly, placed a Milky Way bar on her TV tray table, and headed for the back door. "Grandmother, you're the best. We've got to do this more often."

Rachel was standing at the back gate when he crossed the yard, and she whispered into his ear: "What did she say?"

"Damned if I know."

"I know!" Rachel said knowingly. "I hate when she does that."

## Chapter 19: Reverse Engineering

    Throughout the following week, John poured over the thirteen thumb drives and returned to Mac's website several times. Regardless of which way anybody's winds were blowing, Grandmother Renee was right about one thing. It didn't matter whether Mac wanted to be found or not. What mattered most to him was whether or not she was crazy in a dangerous sort of way. She had found out everything there was to know about him, and she had done most of it with a computer. The thumb drives held all the secrets to that nifty trick, and, one by one, he was using them all to research the mysterious Sean McKnight.
    John was impressed by the Hunter-Seeker, LLC website's list of companies for whom Mac had found employees. It was a miniature Who's Who of America's top corporations, side-by-side with hundreds of small businesses which may have been known only in their own backyards, but paid her the same percentage-of-initial wages as the big dogs. Mac was by no means indigent.

"Plan A" reimbursement for employees hired was 25% of annual salary upon signing. "Plan B" was 10% of annual salary upon signing, and 5% per paycheck for six months...even if the employee quit or was fired. This option also included a 5% credit toward the next time that company used Mac's service. "Plan C" was 5% on signing, and 5% per paycheck for one year, even if the employee quit or was fired, and a 10% credit for the next time. The money was good, the freedom was incredible, and the redhead was clearly nobody's fool.

As he plied her various sources for birth documents, school records, media, etc., John watched Mac's life unfold before his eyes. She had been spot-on about the similarities in their personalities, but she had failed to mention the vast dissimilarities in their upbringing. Her father, Edward McKnight, was the last in a long line of the Baltimore McKnights whose business prowess, from clear back in the 1700's, helped put the port city on the map. The McKnights attended the right schools, sat on the right boards, and belonged to the right yacht and country clubs. They lived and thrived in the limelight, periodically held just the right military and/or political posts, and possessed a polished PR pedigree that seemed to positively sparkle...until young Sean hit adolescence.

John was sobered to see that personality quirks which had been lovingly embraced in his own younger years, brought severe repercussions in Mac's. She was never a joiner, refusing both sports and the fine arts. Her parents were increasingly alarmed by her tendency to disappear, and her first time in the newspaper was after being charged with trespassing. She had created a sanctuary for herself in an absentee neighbor's carriage house, and despite having cleaned it thoroughly, probably the first spring cleaning it had undergone in a decade, the neighbors returned from Europe just to press charges. The local paper certainly must have enraged Mac's family more by mentioning that there had been long-standing bad blood between Edward McKnight and the neighbors who claimed he had cheated them on a business deal.

As it became apparent that money alone could no longer get Sean into the right schools, and that neither Harvard nor Yale were in the cards for her, things got really nasty. According to the newspaper and the online police blotter from the time, Mac had disappeared for an extended period, and after an extensive hunt for her proved fruitless, she was subsequently arrested for trespassing again. A boater, cruising Baltimore's Inner Harbor just after sunset, thought he saw movement in the upper rigging of the *U.S.S. Constellation* and called the Harbor Patrol on his ship's radio. Police were notified and dispatched to the museum where they swarmed onto the 1854 Sloop of War and discovered a teenage girl asleep in the crow's nest. Charges were dismissed when an undisclosed deal with prosecutors was reached. To his great dismay, John discovered that the day after the arrest, Mac was admitted to the Young Adult Unit at the Sheppard and Enoch Pratt Psychiatric Hospital, and placed on suicide watch.

After a night of troubled sleep, John arrived at work to find a celebration in progress. Streamers and balloons were hung from the suspended ceiling, and there was a table of goodies spread out in the lobby. In the center was a large sheet cake decorated with the word "CONGRATULATIONS!"

"It's about time you retired," John said to his boss as they met in the hallway.

"In your dreams, young Ghostwalker!" Abraham said with a genuinely hearty laugh. "I'm just getting started! There's a bit of a political issue, but they loved our proposal, and everyone's on board to press ahead."

"What's the catch?" John asked.

"In the end, it's always about cutting up the pie," Abraham said, "and this is a high profile pie, but Frank Ghary is a savvy guy, and his solution sounds brilliant to me. Apparently, the only way Jacobs & Associates and

Coral Gables Construction could bake these apples alone would be if the City of Miami Beach opened a whole new project file. That would mean an extended bid process, and the chance that we'd end up with nothing much beyond the consultation fee. But because the final phase of the original project permit doesn't legally run out until December, Ghary suggested that a new addition be made to the existing project, thus avoiding all the risks and delays."

"What does that mean for us, and for the Coral Gables Construction guys?"

"A smaller, but guaranteed piece of the pie. We subcontract for Frank Ghary, and they subcontract for the current builder."

"Makes sense," John said. "Who's over at the Towers today?"

"I sent the FIU intern so nobody would feel like they're being excluded from the party."

"If you don't mind," John said, "I need to check on a couple of things over there, so I'll send her back for some cake and ice cream."

"Fine with me," Abraham said. "You're kind of a party-pooper anyway, and she's way better looking!"

## Chapter 20: Knock Three Times

    Sometimes John's systematic and logical mind threw him a curveball. It felt like a door swinging open suddenly where only a solid wall had existed before. Sunshine poured through, bringing a moment of clarity that always caught him off guard. After tossing and turning restlessly all night, he had awakened with two things clear in his mind. First, finding out that Mac had been committed to a mental institution should have given him greater pause than he had already been feeling. Instead, he longed to hold her in his arms and celebrate who she was. He loved her. Go figure. The second glimpse of clarity had to do with his "apartment" at the new Brickell Town Towers. He knew, somehow, that he had to finish it for her. Just for her.
    Though he hadn't realized this about himself before, John woke up knowing that he was terrified of sharing his living space with Mac. But it was recognizing the desperate need for sanctuary he was seeing in her life history that

helped him to recognize it in himself. He grew up in dozens of warm and loving households, on sofa beds, in guest rooms, or, more often, sharing a bedroom with adoptive siblings, but from his earliest memories, he had longed for a sanctuary space of his own. John had been capable of accomplishing quite a lot in his short life, but it resonated in him only now how much restorative strength he drew from retreating to his own secret, private place when each busy day was concluded. No matter how well he seemingly handled it all on the outside, dealing with people in the real world was stressful and exhausting on the inside, and without the various sanctuaries he had instinctively built into his life, John now suspected that he too might have ended up in a psychiatric facility.

One of the interesting consequences of tinkering with the blueprints for the Brickell Town Towers project had, until now, lacked significance to John. Suddenly, it was a most convenient revelation. Focused as he was on his sixteenth floor "apartment," he had given no thought to the fact that the finishing changes he had instituted had been automatically applied to each of the nine residential floors below that. He had unintentionally created ten potential secret apartments instead of just one. The top floor, he had decided that morning, would "belong" to Mac. The logical side of his brain knew that he might never see her again, let alone convince her to move to Brickell to be near him, but his heart was telling him that this sanctuary must be built for her. Perhaps, like Kevin Costner's cornfield baseball diamond, if he built it, she would come.

Having made up his mind, John now had to shift his eclectic collection of recycled paraphernalia down to the fifteenth floor. That would require both deconstruction and new construction on the floor below. He had accomplished those tasks quite easily while the construction crews were still finishing up, but now, even with his unlimited access, John had to be very careful. The grand opening was two weeks away, the first floor retail shops were already open, and some of the commercial offices on floors two through six were already up and running. Many of the residential apartments had been rented, and on the first of the month, people would begin moving in. Everyone was used to seeing him come and go, and as the construction crews gave way to the painters and then to the flooring installers, he was glad to see how quickly folks chose to assume that he was renting an apartment there himself. The building superintendent posed the greatest challenge, and John made it his business to avoid any protracted conversation that might lead to uncomfortable questions. He was there before all the rest of them, so he seemed to them almost like part of the interior decoration. And that had served him well so far.

Carrying a battery powered reciprocal saw in his backpack was a challenge. Even without the blade installed, the tool protruded out from under the pack's closure flap. Add to that the hammer, the electric screwdriver, the hinges, the hand vac, the magnetic closures, and painter's tape, and it looked more like he was hauling St. Nick's satchel. He had long since repositioned the fixed security camera on the top floor, but now he would need to do the same thing on the fifteenth floor...weeks after a security firm had been hired and the system had gone live. He took one last look at the fifteenth floor's camera point of view from his secret monitor screen on the top floor, and then headed down the exterior fire escape stairway on the building's northeast corner with his heavy backpack on his shoulders, a plastic milk crate in one hand, and shiny gold key in the other. This was only one of several keys he had acquired during the building's construction. Being able to disarm the alarm and come and go freely on that stairway was part of his grand design.

He was pretty sure that he could open the fire door halfway without the top corner of the door intersecting the camera's view. As he eased it open, he prayed he was right, and slid the milk crate in and around the partially open door. Next, he carefully squeezed himself in and around until he too was directly below the camera. On the floor above, John had actually remounted the fixed camera closer to the ceiling, puttied up the old screw holes, and waited for the painting crew to come through and erase the evidence of his tampering. Here however, the wall was freshly painted, and any movement of the bracket would be obvious. Instead, he would slowly tip the camera upwards, until, hopefully, it no longer showed that section of the hallway into which he was then going to cut a new doorway like the one he had carved out upstairs long before new paint and security cameras were an issue. Standing on the milk crate, he loosened the screws and began edging the front of the camera upwards so slowly that its movement was hopefully imperceptible to the security guard in the lobby, should he glance at the monitor. Five minutes later, his shoulders aching, John retightened the screws and snuck back upstairs to check his progress on his own monitor. There was a lot more ceiling in the shot now, and there was one less legitimate apartment door visible on the north side of the long hallway, so, in theory at least, he could proceed.

One of John's most celebrated alterations' to the Towers was its residential hallway scheme. His changes were cheap, easy, and visually remarkable. With actual video footage, he demonstrated how cold and institutional the typical off-white residential hallway looked, as compared to that of the average middle to high class hotel, and proposed a simple solution that involved inexpensive pine crown molding. Wall treatment made all the difference in the world, and simply by creating a rectangular picture frame on the wall between each apartment door, and painting it to match the doors, rather than the wall, the hallway looked and felt more like an art gallery than a hospital corridor. The ownership consortium was thrilled. Not-so-coincidentally, the "picture frame" in the smaller wall section between the last apartment door on the north wall of each floor, and the fire escape door ended up being the same height as all the others, but exactly the same width as a standard 2-foot, 8-inch door.

There was a 35-inch gap in the concrete wall forms, and it was framed with 2"X 4" pine to facilitate drywall installation. By the time John was lending a helping hand to the carpentry crew framing off the apartment doorways and these ten small gaps, no one thought anything of it. Once the wall treatment was up and painted, he placed painter's tape around the inner edge of the "picture frame" so as not to mar the paint job with splintering, used a reciprocal saw with a fine toothed blade to pop out his "doorway," and then he reinforced it with 1" X 2" cedar furring and hung it on interior hinges with an invisible magnetic door closure. The result was a completely invisible door, not unlike Harry Potter's dormitory entrance, but instead of a magical password, he needed only to press firmly in the area of the magnetic closure device, and the door/"picture" popped open and swung out from its crown molding "frame." Like the bulkhead doorway of a ship, one needed to step up into this doorway, but the inconvenience weighed against the free rent and total privacy was hardly worth noting; and, fortunately, ADA wheelchair accessibility standards need not apply.

## Chapter 21: Fit for a Queen

At the same time, he began to consider how he would furnish Mac's secret penthouse. John knew instinctively that dumpster diving was not going to cut it. Broken wheelchairs and old fishing nets were probably not the way to a woman's heart, but something about IKEA didn't seem right either. His compromise came in the form of an auction house in Boca Raton that held weekly estate sales. Giving pricey old items a second lease on life was somehow satisfying, and the auctions themselves were quite entertaining.

The "apartment" was a 350 square foot square, with a tapered entrance hallway that gave it the overall appearance of a block font comma. Once a tiny bathroom and an efficiency kitchen were framed in against the east wall, along with a small closet, there wasn't much room for furniture. John created his own take on the "Murphy" concept so that the queen sized bed folded up against the west wall during the day, and disappeared behind a set of sliding bookshelves. Because the building's electrical, water, drain, and air conditioning conduits ran vertically along the wall adjacent to the external fire stairway, access to all four was a breeze.

The north wall, the top of the "comma," was his masterpiece. On the far side of the Towers, the south exterior wall had a 6-foot by 7-foot screened and louvered vent on each floor. These vents allowed for regulation of the air pressure changes whenever the elevators went up or down. To make the vents more visually pleasing, a faux balcony railing was installed under each, in line with all the real balconies on that side of the building. The space John was renovating on the north side, matched identical space on the south side of the hallway, but there it served as service access for the elevators, and had a real door in each hallway. Inserting the same vents and faux balconies on the north side of the building just created continuity of design. John carefully cut "his" and "Mac's" vents into four vertical sections, hinged a pair of these together on either side of the opening, and thus created a set of bi-fold doors leading to somewhat stunted, but very real, balconies. He added handles to each panel, allowing them to open or close the louvers at will. The view of downtown Miami and Biscayne Bay was spectacular.

John's first auction treasure was an antique drop-leaf hall table. Even with the leaf extended, it fit perfectly in the widest end of the entry hall, just beneath the small computer monitor which he had rigged to show whether the hallway was clear so that the secret door could be opened undetected. He added a small crystal vase and a silk rose as the first thing Mac would see should she ever come back into his life. He had used left over mullet netting from his room over Nate's shop in the queen sized Murphy bed frame on the top floor, and covered that with a discarded mover's quilt which he had washed thoroughly. After moving both to the duplicate bed one floor below, he created a lattice structure in the fold-up box upon which he could place a real mattress for Mac. This posed something of a dilemma.

With the help of a rental van and a recycled hand truck, getting two commodes, sinks, motel refrigerators, and even two small electric stove/oven units up thirty two flights of steps was doable, albeit exhausting. A queen sized mattress was something else again. John researched the topic thoroughly, and discovered that something called a "memory foam" mattress was often vacuum-packed for shipping. With all the air sucked out of it, the seven inch thick model came rolled up looking and hefting more like an area rug than a traditional mattress. Once released from its sealed plastic wrappings, it took 24 to 48 hours to resume its normal thickness. This item he had shipped to the Blackfeather's, another obstacle overcome.

He was chagrinned at how easily he was warming up to the idea of having the kind of creature comforts Mac was used to. Walking away from these two squatter dwellings, should that ever prove necessary, would be a little costly, but he was a man on a mission. As he continued to track Mac's life history in the ether, the pace was intolerable to his little sister. Rachel clearly saw John as a man avoiding the mission at all cost, and in an effort to motivate and/or infuriate him, she began to text him. Each day she crafted a textual sharp stick and poked him with it. John Ghostwalker was the master of selective focus, so he largely ignored her wireless barbs. After all, he had something of a plan that had something to do with eventually traveling to the Keys, somehow befriending a random sheriff's deputy, and then hopefully getting a demonstration of the Monroe County T.I.F. system in which they would somehow happen to search for a blue and white Mini-Cooper.

Of course he was not an idiot. So the more ignoring Rachel forced him to focus on his long term "plan," the more ludicrous that plan became. In fact, he admitted to himself one day, it sucked. He was neither a networker nor a schmoozer, and he had never walked up and deliberately befriended a stranger in his life. If a stranger were being mugged by four hooligans, he conceded, only then was he apt to step up and get to know them. Otherwise, not so much. So, in true Ghostwalker form, he came up with a Plan B. John began to contemplate how he might sneak into a Monroe County Sheriff's station, hack into the T.I.F. system, and find Mac himself. Even as this brilliant concept began to unravel under the weight of its own levels of denial, Rachel came up with a textual Plan B of her own.

She would begin her freshman year at the University of Miami in the fall, and had decided to get a BSEd degree. She wanted to be an elementary school teacher. At this moment in his life, her brilliant, doctorate holding adopted brother was behaving in what she considered a very childlike way, so she drew up a simple lesson plan which utilized demonstration rather than lecture. She would show rather than tell John how to overcome his innate insecurities about confrontation and communication. On Monday she sent a picture of Grandmother Renee's favorite orchid in bloom. The accompanying text read: "her favorite plant." Tuesday's picture showed John's room over her dad's shop, and said: "new bedspread i found 4 u at garage sale." Wednesday was Dan Stone watching TV in his little apartment, and read: "first a real address, and now cable TV!" And so, day after day, Rachel simply exemplified non-threatening, but highly informative and interesting communication, a texting primer which she hoped, over time, might erode John's "slippery slope" mentality about the subject.

## Chapter 22: A Picture's Worth a Thousand Words

There were 50 copies of the Sunday paper stacked in the lobby at Jacobs & Associates the following Monday morning. Rick Daboul's composite picture of the "Maestro's Sky Mall" as it would appear in the New World Symphony Hall appeared on the front page of the *Miami Herald*, under a headline reading: "Miami Architect Creates Sky Mall out of Thin Air." Mandy the receptionist was a bit short with him as she told him that the boss was at a meeting with city planners, and that there was a pile of yellow phone call memos on his desk. People wanted to interview him. Local magazine writers, radio talk show and television news program producers, and even a stringer for *Architectural Digest* had called him. Amid congratulatory comments from other associates, John worked his way back towards the men's room until he was sure no one was following him, and then slipped out the fire escape door and disappeared down the alley.

By the time he settled onto a shady bench in Alan Morris Brickell Park, his heart rate had come down some, but his anxiety was still on the rise. He felt like a prison escapee in the woods at night with dancing flashlight beams and baying hounds close behind. The desire to disappear was an old familiar feeling, but it had never been accompanied by loneliness before. He fumbled with his cell phone for a couple moments before holding it at arm's length, snapping a picture of himself, adding a text message that read "me hiding out at amp park," and sending it to Mac.

Somewhere inside him a dam broke. John walked across the street and let himself into his old room at the parking garage. He climbed the ladder, pushed open the hatch, and took a picture of the empty space. The accompanying text message said: "moved out." He sent it to Mac. At the Brickell Town Towers, he shot a picture of his apartment there and added "new digs" before sending it out. Then he went upstairs and took three pictures of Mac's room. The entryway shot of the silk rose said "upstairs, yours." The next said "bed, bath & beyond," and the last, of him on her balcony said: "ur view. i miss u." John collapsed into the wing back office chair he had bought her at the last auction, leaned one elbow on the half-size antique roll-top desk, and stared longingly at his cell phone, willing it to beep. When it did, his hands shook so badly he could barely press the right buttons to bring up the text. Under a picture of Mac's smiling face it said: "me 2."

The oceanfront house on Duck Key had been vacant since the credit crisis/real estate bubble bust. Its owners, who had hoped to retire there, had, like more than a dozen owners in the small island community, tried to refinance when their home's value halved overnight and their property taxes and hurricane insurance premiums had both been doubled. President Obama made it difficult for the recently bailed out banks to refuse such applications, but he had done nothing to keep them from burying trapped owners in months of meaningless requests for additional meaningless information before sending out form letters about how sorry they were to have to deny the owner's application to refinance at current rates. Like so many other American homeowners who had been forced to watch their tax dollars bail out the very crooks who had swindled them out of their retirement nest eggs, they had no choice but to walk away in the face of foreclosure, and resign themselves to decades of working, renting, and ruined credit.

Banks were flush, so the dead real estate market mattered not to them. Unlike the former owners of the homes whose deeds now belonged to them, they were burdened by neither taxes nor insurance premiums. They could easily wait it out, and then unload all the free properties when the market eventually rebounded. It was all profit to them. So Mac felt no twinge of conscience squatting in the thieves' den, even though she grieved for the devastated former owners. The master bedroom faced the Atlantic Ocean, its eastern wall was all windows and sliding glass doors. Mac had chosen this room for her office/yoga studio. Her bed filled the tiny cupola in the living room's open ceiling. She could just barely stretch out fully, but it reminded her of those summer nights sleeping in the crow's nest of the U.S.S. Constellation. Her only pleasant childhood memory was learning to sail, and the time she got to spend out on the water, alone in one of the yacht club's little one-man racing sloops, was as close to perfect as she thought life could possibly get. That John had built her a room, her own room, with a view of the ocean from a beautiful handmade bed was the most romantic thing she could imagine.

The text messages and pictures from John had been the most amazing surprise. Mac had spent the intervening weeks drowning in embarrassment and self-loathing. She had, for the first time in her lone wolf life, attempted to pursue deep feelings for another human being. It felt awkward and unnatural, but she had been irresistibly drawn to John Ghostwalker. It had all been going wonderfully, like a dream, until the inevitable day came when she knew she had to tell him the rest of the story. Admitting, out loud, that she had been stalking him was devastating for her, more so than she could ever have imagined. Mac had spent years fighting off her parents' projections of mental illness. When she was seventeen, they had committed her to a mental hospital against her will, and publically proclaimed their projected diagnosis. It took her months to find a doctor who would stand up for her in the face of that diagnosis and the money behind it. And even after she had won her release and run far away from the family who had betrayed her so many times, the doubts and fears about her sanity swirled just below the surface of her consciousness. Always she refused to give those dark thoughts credence...until she publically proclaimed herself a stalker. Everybody knows that stalkers are crazy.

She would never have faulted John for not reaching out to her. That would have been the most sensible thing for him to do. But he had reached out. And, he had obviously been thinking about her and laboring on her behalf long before that. If love was a rare and precious thing for "normal" people to experience, how much more so, she wondered, must it be for peculiar "thumb drive" people like herself and John Ghostwalker? Mac was too smart to believe it was *fait accompli* for them, but now, at last, there was hope.

## Chapter 23: Trip the Limelight Fandango

His life was suddenly a circus with at least three rings demanding his participation in a performance of some kind. John felt certain that he could not have managed that week without Mac's friendship and the simple, well grounded humanity of his Miccosukee family. When he and Mac showed up together for the Sunday picnic, the neighborhood smiled with one kindly, knowing smile, and the sense of community celebration exceeded those he'd experienced when he was accepted at Haskell or had earned his doctorate degree at FIU. Everyone acted as if nothing had happened, but the joyous warmth that came from seeing two people so obviously in love was palpable.

As much as Mac had fallen in love with the secret apartment John had built and furnished for her, the Miccosukee neighborhood stole her heart just as completely. Rachel felt like the sister she never had, she could never have imagined feeling so comfortable with, nor so welcomed by, so many people at once, and Grandmother Renee was absolutely irresistible.

"You are back from calling the winds, my child, and your wind was favorable for us all," the wizened little woman said with a grin when Mac bent to embrace her. "I am glad."

"I am too, Grandmother," Mac said, throwing a puzzled glance in John's direction.

John shrugged his ignorance and leaned in to kiss the venerable woman's head. "We are all glad about the winds, Grandmother," he said, "now what can I get you to eat?"

The afternoon was so emotionally refreshing for John and Mac that they sat in contented silence as the Mini-Cooper carried them back into Brickell. Mac found a parking spot behind the Towers, and they walked up the fire stairs hand-in-hand.

"How did you know to do this for me?" Mac asked as John walked her to her invisible door.

John slipped off his backpack, pulled out Mac's cigar box, and handed it to her. "It's all in the thumb drives."

Mac opened the familiar box and found that there were fourteen numbered drives inside.

"Guess that means I'm a stalker too," John said as he opened her door. "Hope that's OK with you."

"I'll let you know in the morning," Mac said, and for the first time, she pulled him through the doorway with her and closed it behind him.

As the sunlight warmed the west wall and shone on Mac's sleeping face, John Ghostwalker's mind was already chasing itself around in circles. The emotions of love, tenderness, excitement, fear, uncertainty and joy had swirled around and through them both throughout that most remarkable evening, but John, always an early riser, woke to find the extraordinary feelings being replaced by his more linear and logical thoughts. He knew instinctively that he must leave. Not only because of his job, but because they were both very private people who required sanctuary in the same way all humans required air. It would be most practical if he slipped out quietly before Mac woke, probably best for both of them, but as the sun lit the skin of her shoulders and the side of her face, all the emotions crowded back in and he longed to embrace her. For a long while he was paralyzed between these two profoundly powerful aspects of his being, and he began to reach out several times, only to pull back his hand at the last second.

At last, he slipped out of bed, quietly pulled on his clothes, and wrote "I love you!" on a paper towel. This he placed on the edge of Mac's pillow along with the silk rose from the hall table. Checking the wall monitor, he pulled inwards on the door to release the magnetic springs, and he stepped out into the hallway. Along with all the overwhelming feelings of love, there was also, in that moment, a very comforting feeling of relief. His rote morning routine had never been so difficult to manage, and he walked right past the door to Jacobs & Associates, only realizing what he had done as he began to cross the less familiar intersection at the other end of the block. Mandy Hawkins, the receptionist, was barely trying to conceal her amusement when he came back by the front windows from the opposite direction and walked in the glass door.

"Practicing your lines?" Mandy said, handing him a memo pad sheet when he approached her desk, making a tiny noise behind her hand that almost sounded like a snort.

"My lines for what?"

"Your interview for *Architectural Digest* this morning." She pointed to the memo in his hand. "She's already in your office with a tape recorder and a photographer."

"Shit!" John said as looked at the paper upon which Mandy had written "Sherry Langston."

"I wouldn't lead with that," Mandy quipped, "but

maybe save it for your big finish."

"Thanks," he said, heading down the hall like a condemned man on his way to the gas chamber.

"*De nada*," she replied, and this time he was certain she had snorted.

Mac woke up slowly and stretched like a cat in the warm beams of sunlight that covered her bed. The light danced and glistened on Biscayne Bay in the distance, and far below her, the sounds of the city wafted up like the beat of music she could not quite make out. She read John's note, and held the rose against her chest while she padded across the small room to return it to its vase. While she made coffee, she thought back on how amazing and beautiful the night had been. For years she had spurned numerous would-be lovers because she knew instinctively that she simply would not want them in her space the next morning. She had come to the conclusion that, having almost lost him, she could somehow make John the exception. She would try to overcome her strange need for privacy. In truth, finding him gone when she awoke was every bit as satisfying as the physical intimacy had been. John just got her. She didn't have to explain nor defend herself. Respect was the foundation of his love, and because in her past she had only experienced "love" that was conditional, she found that deeply satisfying, even more than a bit erotic.

Mac had been worried when she first moved in and saw how tiny her room was. Her initial fear was that she would have to give up Yoga, but when John showed her how to fold her bed up against the wall and slide the two bookshelves together over it, she very quickly came to love the place. The flat screen HD TV was mounted on the bathroom door at the foot of her bed, and the tiny kitchen had everything she could imagine needing. The closet was definitely a "man closet," but she'd never had much interest in wardrobe. Mac never met her clients, nor the employees she located for them, and her social life had been non-existent for years before John. The closet would do just fine. The small roll-top desk was exquisite, and for a career which revolved entirely around her laptop computer, it was much more than adequate.

Having been arrested twice, and questioned on a number of more recent occasions, Mac was more cognoscente of the legal issues surrounding the squatter's life. Not having John's electronic engineering skills, she had always paid for cable and utilities in her own name, so if she was ever "caught," it was easier to explain away her presence as a "misunderstanding." But the draw, the rush she got out of using/beating "the system" without doing any real harm to anyone was based on a deep seeded belief that two percent of the world's population got disproportionally rich from the blood, sweat and tears of the other ninety-eight percent. "They" cheated "us" every chance they got, and then they even went so far as to buy our "public servants" away from us, thus buying a never-ending string of legislation that created even more chances for them to cheat us. The shrink said she was, "acting out against her father," to which she had replied: "No, I'm acting out against all the rich, lying bastards, *including* my father!"

## Chapter 24: Ding Dong

    Having his "story" in *Architectural Digest* as that of a "rising star" and a "wiz kid" was bad enough, but the photo part was even more mortifying. John had arrived at work that day looking and acting more like a spacey hip-hop skater boy than a doctor of architectural design, and the stringer's clingy silk blouse with too few buttons hadn't exactly helped him get his mind off the night before. Abraham Jacobs was thrilled, however, and had taken to calling him "the kid," a label in which his fellow associates took great delight.
    His boss' heady mood dimmed somewhat when a round trip airline ticket to Los Angeles arrived for John, along with an invitation to dinner from Frank Ghary. Mr. Jacobs seemed, suddenly, to be shadowing John around the office, showing far too much interest in John's life, work, and well-being.
    "Enough!" John said, finally exasperated. "Will you stop? I don't even want to go. Here, take the ticket! I'll

even pay the conversion fee."

That might have gone better under different circumstances. The not-too-muffled laughter up and down the hallway, the pig-like snort from the reception desk, and the terrifying notion that John might actually refuse the invitation, didn't exactly improve his boss' state of paranoia.

"No, no!" he said desperately. "You must go. You represent all of us, and it's a great honor, but...." He sputtered to a silent stop.

"I'm not interested in another job," John said, "if that's what you're worried about. I worked too hard to get here so that I could take your job to blow it all on some Hollywood bit part."

Nobody even tried to muffle their laughter this time, and the snorts came in bursts for so long that even Abraham Jacobs started laughing, patted John on the shoulder, and retreated to his office at the end of the hall. The workload had doubled as a result of the New World Center project getting so much attention, and John liked being the go-to guy whose ideas were respected. He still longed to design a great building one day, but for now, the Sky Mall, and the attention it had brought with it, was more than enough for his anxiety level. He wasn't at all thrilled at the prospect of flying to LA, in fact, he had never flown anywhere, and wasn't sure he wanted to. But, once again, real life was dragging him out of his shell. He told himself he could manage the flight if Mac would accompany him, and determined to ask her that evening.

"Hello, Ms. McKnight," said the unfamiliar voice on Mac's cell phone. "My name is Oscar Wright, of Wright, Paglia & Adams, attorneys at law in Baltimore. I am very much aware of your estrangement from your family, so I realize that you may be unaware of your mother's passing. I am sorry for your loss."

Mac's breath caught in her throat. She had never

pondered how this inevitable news would, or would not, affect her, but she had certainly assumed the occasion itself would be decades in the future. "Your firm did not represent my father the last time I knew anything about it," she said finally.

"Nor do we at present," replied Oscar Wright, Esq., "nor will we in the future. I represent your mother."

Mac actually laughed. "My father would never permit my mother to hire her own attorney!"

"That is a true enough statement, Ms. McKnight, but for our purposes, anyway, we should insert the word 'knowingly.' He would never knowingly permit your mother to hire her own attorney. But she did. In point of fact, she hired me the day after your father made her sign your commitment papers."

The sturdy office chair felt like it was wobbling beneath her, and Mac slid off it and let herself down onto the Persian throw rug John had purchased for her at the Boca auction house. "Why would she do that?"

"That cruel act, directed as punishment towards both of you, was the proverbial straw, Ms. McKnight, and your mother finally found just enough strength to begin fighting back. She was a terribly abused woman, to the end of her days, and told me often that the cancer was setting her free, but, as my grandmother would say, 'she discovered her inner mama bear.'"

"That's all well and good, Mr. Wright," Mac said, "but what does it have to do with me?"

"Everything. The day after you were committed to the Sheppard and Enoch Pratt Psychiatric Hospital, your mother opened a checking account in both of your names, hired me, and then drew up a will wholly independent of the one your father made her sign many years before. Everything she had belongs to you now."

Suddenly the Persian rug felt like a flying carpet, and she leaned against the desk to steady herself. "That can't be good," Mac said after several deep Yoga calming breaths. "Father will not take that lying down."

This time, Oscar laughed. "Sarah said you were a bright

one, and she also said you were the strong one. She died hating herself for not protecting you, for not leaving with you, and what she did in the end was her attempt to make that up to you in some way, but we live in a world of unintended consequences, and whether or not she understood fully what the consequences would be for you, I cannot say for sure. But I will hazard a guess if you will agree to trust me, at least temporarily."

"What do you mean?"

"I am authorized to do whatever I deem best as it relates to your mother and her instructions, right up to having the will probated," he answered, "but to follow this through in your best interest, I'd like you to authorize my controller to withdraw a five hundred dollar retainer, hiring me as your attorney in this matter....at least until we've had a chance to speak, in greater depth, about the bigger, nastier picture here. Attorney client privilege will be of great benefit to both of us, I think."

"I really don't care about the money anyway," Mac said. "So do whatever you want."

"Sarah said that you'd say that too! Hold on please."

Mac listened while Oscar Wright buzzed his secretary and instructed him to put the office controller on the line, and to remain on the line himself as a second witness. Seconds later, a female voice came on.

"Hello, Oscar? Are we good to go?"

"Yes, Denise, thank you. I have Bernie on the line as a witness, and I'd like to introduce you both to Sarah's daughter, Sean McKnight."

They both said hello to her. "Hello," she answered. "Please, call me Mac."

"Am I correct, Mac" Oscar said, "that it is your intention that I withdraw five hundred dollars from Sarah McKnight's estate as a retainer, and that you wish to hire me as your attorney in the matter of your mother's will?"

"Yes," Mac answered, "that's correct."

"Please state your full name, and the current date and time for the record."

Mac complied, and Oscar thanked his staff and bid

them return to their duties.

"Thank you, Mac," Oscar said. "Please know that you can fire me at any moment that suits you, no harm nor foul, but let me say how proud I would be to see this through for both you and for your mother. I became very fond of her, and am somewhat in awe of her tenacity. I know this must sound very unlikely to you, based on what she told me about the family dynamic and her disappointing part in it, but when I think of her, I think of one of the Bible stories my grandmother used to tell me about Samson. May I share it?"

"Please do," Mac said as she returned to her office chair.

"Well, as I'm sure you know, the Philistines hated Samson for his great strength, and with the help of a temptress named Delilah, they were able to cut off his hair, the source of his power, and capture him at long last. To further humiliate their enemy, they poked out Samson's eyes and made him fumble blindly about the public forum for their own entertainment. According to my grandmother, this was a powerful teaching moment for Samson, and no sooner had he owned it and confessed it before his God, than his hair began growing back and a plan came into his mind. He waited until the Philistines next great day of celebration, when everyone was packed into the public forum, and he positioned himself between the two main support pillars of the great stone structure. With all his might, he pushed outwards on those columns, and literally brought the house down...on his enemies, and on himself. Mac, if I may be so bold as to say it, I think your mother's last wish was to give you the power of Samson, in a manner of speaking. What you choose to do with it is your business. My job is to explain your options and to protect your mother's estate until it is safely in your hands."

## Chapter 25: Parting Ways

It was a Parkour night, so finding Mac gone was a surprise, but her note was far more surprising. She was already on a plane bound for Baltimore, where her mother's funeral was being held the following day. She would call when she landed. Every day John learned something new about Mac. While the education was sometimes a tad difficult to come to grips with, he had told her that she reminded him of a beautiful flower that was always blooming, unfolding itself to reveal more and more of its true shape and color. There was nothing boring about her, and perhaps because she had taught him how to embrace his own peculiarities, it was easier for him not to be threatened by hers.

Her concept of money management and banking was a recent case in point. John had been shocked when he returned from the MailBox4U store where she now shared his postal box "suite" with an eight inch tubular package for Mac. While they chatted about their day, she had opened the mailing tube, withdrawn a Pringles potato chip canister, and dumped out several hundred dollars in cash onto her desk. After carefully flattening out the bills, she took a screwdriver out of her kitchen drawer and motioned for him to follow her. She kept right on talking about her latest client as she checked the hallway monitor screen and then proceeded out the door. Mac knelt by the fire extinguisher enclosure on the wall next to the fire escape door, loosened the upper two screws, removed the two lower screws securing the inset red box to the wall, and pulled outwards so that the bottom of the entire enclosure swung out slightly. Reaching up underneath into the concrete cut-out, she retrieved a sandwich sized Zip-Lock bag, whereupon she added her newly flattened cash to the sizable stash of bills already stacked side-by-side in the bag, flattened out the air before resealing it, and returned it to its hiding place. The fire extinguisher box resisted her efforts, but when she replaced the two screws and tightened them down along with the upper set, there was no sign that anything had been tampered with.

"I'm going to have to open a bank branch on your floor," she had laughed, "this one's getting full!"

When he followed her back inside, John asked all the obvious questions and discovered that Mac was probably not as well off as he had first thought. In an effort to remain as off-the-grid as possible, she had explained, hers was strictly a "cash only" business.

"All those clients on your website," he had exclaimed, "they pay you cash?"

"Of course not, silly. They write out their contracted payment checks to my favorite charities."

Still puzzled, John asked: "And who are your favorite charities?"

Mac rolled up the top of her desk and withdrew a sizable check made out to "Equal Educational Opportunities" and two already filled out shipping labels. The one to the charity, she affixed to the mailing tube, the other, a self-addressed label, she dropped into the Pringles canister along with the check.

"The ones who donate some cash back to me," she said as she slipped the potato chip container into the shipping tube and resealed the end with strapping tape. "It turns out that most charitable fund raiser types have a significant petty cash allotment, so I become an anonymous "fund raising expense" on their records, and my client gets a donation write-off. Everybody wins!"

She had handed John the package and asked him to mail it on his way to work the next day.

John's reverie was broken when his cell phone rang. "Hello, Mac! Are you OK?"

"I'm good," she answered. "Just landing. I've got a meeting with a lawyer in the morning, and the funeral's tomorrow night. Apparently my mother left me some money, and Daddy dearest is undoubtedly going to try and invalidate her will."

"Sorry," John said. "Anything I can do?"

"Yes. Fly to LA and make nice with Mr. Ghary."

"How did you know about that?"

"Abraham called me. He's in a tizzy, afraid you're going to freak out on him. You're not, are you?"

"I was hoping you'd come along and hold my hand," John whined.

"Not in the cards, my dear, so pull on your big boy pants and ride, boldly, ride!"

"Why does that sound familiar?"

"James Caan quoting Edgar Allan Poe to John Wayne," Mac replied before going on:

"Over the Mountains
Of the Moon,
Down the Valley of the Shadow,
Ride, boldly ride,"
The shade replied-
If you seek for El Dorado!"

After they hung up, John went upstairs and began to pack his only "suitcase," an oversized backpack he had "recycled" while still in grad school. He rolled his things "military style" as Nate had taught him to do, but wondered what his only suit would look like by the time he arrived in California. This trip exemplified the kind of social customs he felt most uncomfortable with. There were themes underlying themes, and much of the "real" conversation was unspoken. He watched it happen, in movies, on TV, and in the real world, but it felt wrong to him. "Be careful," Grandmother Renee had told him, "anytime a man refuses to say exactly what he means." Since John had no idea how one could recognize this behavior, or exactly how to be careful in those situations, he had chosen to avoid them whenever possible.

Just as he had always drawn solace and strength from privacy, he now felt somehow bereft knowing that Mac was a thousand miles away. Her love had added dimension to his life, and had livened and strengthened his soul in ways he could not have imagined. Like all gifts from Life, the Universe, and Everything, there was a catch, and John suddenly understood the song lyrics much better: "You don't know what you got 'till it's gone."

Mac arrived at the Baltimore Waterfront Hotel and found, as Oscar Wright had promised, three envelopes waiting for her at the reception desk: two number ten business envelopes, and a fat nine by twelve that looked as if it might burst at the seams. Once settled into her room, she followed Oscar's instructions and opened the number ten envelope with his firm's return address on it first.

"Dear Mac," Oscar had written, "the other small envelope is from your mother to you, and no one at the firm has opened it. But since I expect it will explain the large envelope, you should probably read it next. The materials in the large envelope are all copies of items placed in my care by your mother through the years. I made the copies myself, and the originals are in my office safe. I have not shared anything about the contents with anyone, but you and I can discuss them at length in the morning. See you then. – Oscar."

## Chapter 26: Family Ties

"I haven't seen you here before, have I? I take this one all the time, and everybody knows me, and looks after me. Are you from Miami too? My dad runs a non-profit organization called 'Filling Empty Houses' there, and my mom's an actress in Hollywood, well, she wants to be an actress, but she's already done a commercial for toothpaste and an infomercial for an exercise machine. I think she's very pretty, and my dad says I look just like her, but I don't think his new girlfriend likes that we talk about mom so much, so we try to wait until she's not around. Are you divorced? My dad and mom are still friends, and talk all the time, but Jenny's folks really hate each other, and they can't even look at each other. I think I'd rather not be divorced when I grow up, but my folks say that sometimes it's the best thing, but sometimes not. Are you OK?"

John wasn't so OK. The precocious youngster in the seat next to him had been rattling on since the pre-flight safety talk had concluded, and as the engine noise level increased and they taxied towards the runway, he turned and bent towards her. "I guess I'm a little nervous," he whispered in a conspiratorial way. "I've never flown before."

"Oh," she said knowingly, "well I was scared too my first time, but now I do it all the time, and it's really no big deal. It'll get really loud in a minute, but that's just 'till we get off the ground, and after that, you'll hardly notice the noise anymore, and it's almost always very smooth along the way. In fact, in a few hours, like after the movie is done and they give us lunch, we'll be able to see the Grand Canyon 'cause we're on the port side of the plane. Port is left because it's a four letter word too, and starboard is the name for the right side of the plane, well, and for boats too. My name is Katie. What's yours?"

"John," he said quietly as his stomach did flip-flops in time with the increasing RPM's of the engines.

"OK, John," Katie said, "let's do this." She reached into her purse, pulled out one of those tiny game machines he'd seen kids use, always wondering how their thumbs could move so fast. She reached out across the arm rest with her left hand and took his right hand in her own, and then held out the game machine between them with her right. "It's called 'Thaxiss.' You catch the red bubbles and I'll catch the blue ones. Go!"

John instinctively grabbed the device with his left hand and began manipulating the joystick/button with his thumb, imitating Katie as she swept a little blue net around the tiny screen capturing flying bubbles with it. When he finally caught his first red bubble and shouted "Got one!" a little too loudly, he realized that they were airborne, and that the engine roar was all-but-gone.

"See," Katie said as she put the toy back into her bag, "that wasn't so bad, was it?"

"No, Katie, thanks to you, it wasn't bad at all."

Mac hadn't slept a wink, and when her cab dropped her

off at Wright, Paglia & Adams, she looked it. Bernie reintroduced himself as Mr. Wright's secretary, and asked Mac what she took in her coffee as he ushered her into Oscar's office.

"Good morning, Mac!" Oscar said. "How was your flight?"

"Better than last night's sleep," she answered. "You sure know how to stir up a person's life."

"Well, to be fair, I'm only the messenger," he said as Bernie reentered with Mac's coffee. "This is your mom's hot potato that we're tossing around."

"Thank you," Mac said to Bernie, who nodded and closed the door after himself when he left.

"Not to pry," Oscar said, "but I'm assuming your mother had some master plan for the, shall we say, *sensitive*, documents she gave into my keeping? When she passed, and I opened my envelope, her instructions were to personally make copies for you, and to prepare the originals for automatic shipment to the state attorney general's office in the event of any harm coming to you or to myself. That, of course, was a bit unsettling, so as an officer of court, I chose not to read them in any depth, but even a cursory glance while photocopying them made it obvious that your father probably wouldn't be thrilled to know that we have them."

"My God," Mac said, "you got that right. I always knew my father was shady, and did business with shady characters, but I was clueless about how shady the shade really was. I'm no lawyer, but I'm guessing mom was right. That stuff could put him behind bars for a long time."

"That's what I was thinking too," Oscar said, "but what does she want you to do with it?"

"Well, that's the strangest thing. She never said. She apologized to me, over and over. She obviously hated him, and herself, but she only referred to the documents as 'insurance,' saying that I should have them now."

"Now we're back to my initial suspicions, and to the story about Samson. Your mom accumulated the strength to bring down the house on your father's head, but instead of doing so, she passed that power to you. And then, instead of suggesting that you do the honors, as I was wrongly assuming she would do, she simply called it 'insurance.' OK, I guess I need to ponder that more, but at present, let me explain the situation that will begin unrolling shortly after the funeral. By the way, will you be attending?"

"I'd rather not."

"I was hoping you'd say that, all things considered. With your permission, I'll send my investigator, just to see who's there. Depending on whether or not your dad knows anything about what Sarah was doing, he may have some of his shady friends looking for you, so not going to the funeral is good, and going back to your hotel is probably not so good. Now I wish I'd read that stuff carefully, and with your permission, I will, but for now, can I send Bernie over to get your things?"

"If you're trying to scare me," Mac said, "it's working. Am I really in danger?"

"I certainly hope not, but your father's law firm has been known to defend folks suspected of having mob ties, and I don't think we should just assume that there's no significance to that. Can I send Bernie over to the Waterfront? He'll bring back your stuff, but we'll let the four day reservation ride in case anyone's watching."

"Sure," Mac said, "but why does that just make me feel worse?"

"I know," Oscar replied, "but let's just hope it's all my overactive imagination at work." He buzzed Bernie, and the door opened promptly. "Bernie, please do me a great favor, and please do it carefully. Mac will give you her room key at the Waterfront. If, and only if, no one is watching you, enter her room, collect her belongings, and return here with them. Take these," Oscar said, handing Bernie the vase of fresh flowers from his desk, "put them in that giant gift bag out in the supply closet. If you get in, leave the flowers and carry Mac's stuff back out in the bag. If anybody seems at all interested in following you upstairs to her floor, place the flowers in front of some other room's door, and then go home and call me from there. Got it?"

"No problem, boss."

"Good. Thanks." Bernie took the flowers and left, and Oscar turned to Mac. "I'll buy you replacement stuff if it comes to that, but suddenly nothing seems routine about any of this. OK, back to the game plan, Mac. Your father may or may not file for a reading of your mother's old will, but since you are not likely to be in it, nor any other party outside of himself, I doubt that he will. His law firm will likely just file it as read. I, on the other hand, must file for a public reading of the more recent will, and that's going to be the bell that signals round one of this fight."

"But why does there have to be a fight?" Mac asked. "Why can't we forget about her will, or give the money to charity, and just go back to our lives?"

"Two reasons," Oscar replied, "that have everything to do with the 'unintended consequences' thing I mentioned the first time we spoke. Reason one, I am legally bound to carry out your mother's wishes. Once I have done so, you will be free to sign it over to the charity of your choice, and, as you say, go back to your life. Reason two, and I just love that you never even asked me about this, would be the six point four million dollars Sarah left you."

## Chapter 27: Hollywood Nights

John landed in LAX knowing more about Katie and her family than he knew about Mac and hers, but the spunky little lady had stolen his heart. He met her mom, Stella, when he and Katie deplaned together, and they all parted as BFF's. Seeing a uniformed driver with a sign that said 'Ghostwalker' on it was as unreal as was his first limo ride. Frank Ghary was a legend, even his own house was studied under descriptions as varied as deconstructionist, Santa Monica School, and California Funk; he knew Hollywood actors and directors, there'd been a documentary movie made about him, he created a jewelry line for Tiffany's, and he traveled the world designing buildings on a regular basis, so John knew that their dinner meeting had to involve some high class restaurant where he would be intolerably under dressed and embarrassingly unable to divine the menu.

"We're stopping at a hotel first, right?" he asked the driver. "I need to clean up and change."

"No," the driver said simply. "I've been instructed to

drop you off at a residence in Santa Monica."

"Shit!"

"What's that?"

"Oh, sorry, nothing," John said, frantically opening his backpack and pulling out his wrinkled suit. The driver tried hard not to laugh as John rolled around in the back seat like a contortionist, scrambling to change his clothes. The result was something along the lines of a Salvation Army homeless look, but fortunately John could only see his hair in the driver's mirror, supercharged as it was with static after his wrestling match with the polyester suit jacket. He re-tied the old shoelace, wishing he had another of Becky Deacon's scrunchies in order to make himself look less scrungy. That was bad enough, and so had he been aware of the overall presentation he was making, he might have remained in the limo, praying for the apocalypse.

Instead, he thanked the driver, handed him a five dollar bill, and got out in front of the house he'd only seen pictures of in text books and architectural magazines. He realized at that moment that had he used chain link fencing instead of a catamaran hull for the roof structure out on Dan Stone's little island in the Everglades, the two homes would look somewhat similar. John reached the oddly unfinished looking front porch, carefully straightened his backbone and his tie, and knocked on the front door.

"Hello," said the very friendly looking women who opened the door, "you must be John. I'm Frank's wife, Berta. Here, let me take those."

Before he could react, she had deftly taken his pack, whisked off his tie, unbuttoned his top shirt button, and helped him out of his suit coat. "I'll just hang them here," she said, indicating a wall-mounted hat and coat rack in the shape of a large fish. "The boys are in the den, just follow the noise." Berta gently shoved him down the hallway and returned to the kitchen.

"The boys," three of them, were dressed in jeans and t-shirts, and were sitting and/or standing here and there around the room, gesticulating at and talking enthusiastically to the wall mounted television. The general theme of their cacophony had everything to do with the Los Angeles Kings and the Toronto Maple Leafs.

"Sit!" said the grey-haired 82-year-old "boy," patting the sofa next to his recliner. "You're cheering for Toronto, by-the-way...I'm outnumbered here. My sons, that's Sami," Frank Ghary said, pointing to the other end of the sofa, "and that's Alejandro," he said, gesturing at the young man standing just to the side of the TV, making slap shot motions with an invisible hockey stick, as if to telepathically urge the skating player on the screen to follow suit. "This is John Ghostwalker." Both men turned to John, waved, and said "hello" before returning their rapt attention to the game. "One would think they'd honor their father's heritage, but no, they're all about the Kings!"

He nodded and waved to no one in particular, then turned back to Ghary, whose t-shirt was adorned with the picture of a house in Berkeley John had seen online. It was shaped like a great silver fish, was reportedly a very green design, and was constructed primarily out of recycled materials. "Thanks for the kind invitation and the transportation," John said. "It's been very exciting having the chance to work with you."

"Thank you," Ghary said, "but you're doing all the working. I'm just riding along on your coattails!"

The buzzer sounded halftime, and Berta swept into the den with a tray of sandwiches and a bowl of chips. Alejandro and Sami disappeared, only to return with a selection of bottled beverages, a freezer ice cube container, and five mismatched glasses. To John, it all felt very much like Monday Night Football at Nate's. He laughed at himself for all his fearful projections about a fancy night on the town.

"Frank tells me that you are very talented, John," Berta said, offering him a paper plate and then the sandwich tray. "He says you think outside the box, and that's how he divides up the whole profession."

"There are lots of guys in the box," Frank Ghary added

as he turned down the volume and his family circled around the coffee table. "They are the backbone of the profession, but at its best, architecture is a science *and* an art, and the art gives it its soul." This last line, his sons and his wife said right along with him.

"Dad says that a lot," Sami laughed.

"And most of us outside the box, the dreamers," Ghary went on with a gleeful roll of his eyes, "either never get a chance to build our dreams, or if we do get a chance, it's all too easy to go to the opposite extreme, losing too much function because we have so much of other people's money to spend on artistic form. I must strive for balance, but I agree with my FIU friend, Professor Andrews, who thinks you were born with it."

The lively discussion which ensued was remarkable, and the family dynamic reminded John of home, but when the buzzer announced the second half of the hockey game, Berta began gathering up the leftovers while "the boys" attention returned fully to the television set. John picked up the paper plates, the empty bottles and the freezer tray, and followed Berta into the kitchen.

"Thank you for your hospitality," he said. "I feel very honored, and have enjoyed my visit, but I should probably call a cab and find a hotel."

"Nonsense!" Berta said, startled. "We've already made up the guest room. Frank flies to France tomorrow, so you'll ride to LAX together. It's game night with the boys, a big deal around here as you can see, especially when Frank's Maple Leafs play the Kings, but Frank's not done with you yet! Your room is the last one down that hall on the left and the bathroom's across the way. Anytime you feel like crashing, just go...you must be exhausted."

John enthusiastically helped Frank cheer on the Maple Leafs to a 4-3 victory over LA, and by the time he wearily grabbed his pack from the foyer and headed down the hall to the guest room, he was smiling a very heart-happy smile. The day had been a lesson in what is best about humanity, what is right with the world, and unlike many of the lessons repeated daily on television, in the movies, and all over the newspapers, it left neither fear nor anxiety in its wake. John fell asleep thinking about a Black Eyed Peas song. It had been a good, good night indeed.

The ride to LAX was like five years of grad school, only better. Ghary sometimes reminded him of Grandmother Renee, but was much easier to understand. The legend seemed determined that John not get "sidetracked" by the attention he would receive, not only from the Sky Mall project, but from whatever projects his dream might lead him to experience. "When you start believing your press releases and reviews, or when you try to mold yourself to conform to a persona others create in your name," Ghary told him, "you will begin to lose yourself, and the wheels will begin falling off the bus. Do you understand this idea?"

"I think so," John answered tentatively.

"You are artistic, you are a dreamer, and you are creative, in part, because you come from a more emotional place inside your head and inside your soul. This magic within us usually brings with it certain peculiarities. We are 'odd ducks,' or 'eccentric,' or a host of other labels that 'normal' people concoct to describe us, and if we become embarrassed by our uniqueness, if we shy from it or try to bury it, the magic dies. We become just another *schmuck* in the box."

The car pulled up to the international terminal, the driver opened Ghary's door, and the great architect slapped John on the shoulder as he stepped out onto the sidewalk. "I'll see you in Miami for the Skywalk opening. You've got my cell number, call me anytime. But remember, don't be a *schmuck*!"

## Chapter 28: Dancing with the Devil

Mac's presence at the reading of her mother's will took the form of a high tech plastic tri-pod device on the conference table. That was just as well because, between her father, his gaggle of lawyers, Oscar and Bernie, the small room was crowded. She could watch the proceeding because Oscar was videotaping it for the record, and there was a monitor set up on the desk in front of her, two floors up in an accountant's office. Both the accountant, a personal friend of Oscar's named Fred Hoover, and Oscar's investigator, Seth Lowenstein, were in the office with her. Seth looked like a typical Jewish rabbinical student, wire rim glasses, white shirt, yarmulke, even long sideburns, but Oscar had warned her that in Seth's case, looks were always deceiving.

"He's got some new get-up every week," Oscar had told her. "He really gets off looking non-threatening. And he's an ex-Navy Seal."

Introductions were concluded in the conference room,

Oscar stated for the record that the proceedings were being videotaped, and proceeded to open the sealed envelope containing Sarah McKnight's will. Edward McKnight, looked at the teleconference machine intently when Oscar said that Sean was attending by telephone, and then stared directly into the lens of the video camera with a look so cold it made Fred Hoover shudder.

"I'm so sorry," he said. "I see now why Oscar thought it best that you watch from here."

"That's definitely not his happy look…no, wait, he never had a happy look," Mac said. "I know the man on his left. He was father's lawyer as far back as I can remember, but I don't recognize any of the other guys."

"The serious looking gentleman on his right, the one who limped in with the black crutch thing, was at the funeral last night," Seth said, "and I doubt he's ever been to law school. He does have some authority though, but whether your dad's hiring his own muscle these days, or someone else is hiring muscle to babysit your dad, I don't know yet."

As Oscar began reading the straightforward document, first the lawyer, and then the hired muscle took turns restraining her father's frequent outbursts. The gestures began subtly enough, as a gentle touch on his suit coat sleeve, but by the fourth or fifth time Oscar had paused, politely clearing his throat or taking a drink of water as if he hadn't noticed, the man on Edward McKnight's right had had enough. He calmly reached under the table with his left hand, and Mac's father's eyes went wide with surprise. A sweat appeared on his beet-red face, but he shut up immediately, and Oscar continued his reading of the will as if nothing at all had happened.

"I guess that answers my question," Seth said quietly.

"Holy Mother of God," Fred Hoover said, making the sign of the cross.

When the words "estate in the approximate amount of six point four million dollars" came out of Oscar's mouth, Edward McKnight burst to his feet, knocking his keeper's arm into the edge of the table and, thus, the man's hand off of his knee cap.

"She stole that money! Every penny of it! She had no right to give it away! I'll see you in hell before....."

Whatever he had intended to say was interrupted by, what could only be ascertained later after reviewing the tape in slow motion, a broken thumb. At that instant, however, it looked for all the world like Edward McKnight had simply lost his train of thought and collapsed instantly back into his seat, clutching himself in earnest.

"Do I understand that you will be contesting this will?" Oscar asked the lead counsel.

"It seems there may be some question as to whether Mrs. McKnight had a legal right to appropriate the funds in question," the lawyer said uncertainly, glancing at the handler for support. None was forthcoming, and his associates were a very uncomfortable looking crew.

"Ms. McKnight," Oscar said to the teleconference device, "there seems to be an issue about the legality of the estate funds." Everyone in the room froze and stared at the machine in the middle of the table as he continued. "Did I understand you correctly that, among the private paperwork your mother left in my safe for you, there are documents relating directly to the various business deals and subsequent bank deposits your mother made through the years?"

As she had been instructed by Oscar ahead of time, Mac counted to five before releasing the mute button and speaking into Fred's phone. "That's correct, Oscar. Why?" Seth gave her a thumbs up for her performance.

"Well," Oscar answered thoughtfully, "legally obtained funds are community property inside a marriage, and either partner has a right to save their share, and then to disburse it in any way they see fit at the time of their passing, but in cases like this, where the legality of how the monies were obtained is in question, we can sometimes save everyone the time and expense of drawing up legal charges by asking the state attorney general's office to review the business affairs in question. If it's all up and up, then the will can be executed. If there are irregularities, then the state attorney must take over the matter, and it's out of our hands. And that's just as well, because you'd want no part of it anyway under those circumstances. So, the question is: do you have any objections to my calling the state attorney general's office and asking that they expedite this for us?"

The tension in the conference room was palpable, and the glances passed back and forth so quickly it made Mac dizzy trying to keep up. As instructed, she only counted to three this time. "No, Oscar," she said firmly, "that sounds like a great idea."

"So, gentlemen," Oscar said confidently, "are we in agreement?"

"That won't be necessary" said the man on her father's right as he bent over and retrieved his Canadian crutch from the floor next to his chair. "We're done here."

And with that, they all filed out as if the room was about to burst into flames.

"Didn't I tell you he was good?" Seth said.

"Yes you did," Mac laughed. "You did indeed."

## Chapter 29: Personal Space

    They exchanged phone calls and text messages as they made their separate ways back to Miami, each in awe of the other's experiences. By the time they were into their routines again, a plan was formulating, and John was blown away, not only by the strange and wonderful woman he had fallen in love with, but by the magic that seemed to infuse their friendship. Though he hoped that he covered it well enough, communication, in general, was not his best thing. He always felt that the other person understood more about the underlying rules of conversational interaction, and because of this, John always felt a step or two behind. Life, the Universe, and Everything sometimes felt like a sea of verbal subtext and jargon in which he was never quite up to speed. Hours or even days after a conversation, John would suddenly become aware of the very moment in which he had missed some subtle cue, or perhaps been misled by an inconspicuous omission by the other party, and trudged ineptly onward, largely on his own.

But with him and Mac, it was as if they had their own shorthand language. Not only did they "get" each other, but they were able to hear each other with such simplicity and ease that communication was no more difficult than walking. Better yet, Mac was a master at communicating with strangers, a natural who seemed to understand all the nuances. Because of these, and many other, fascinating qualities Mac exhibited, John was convinced that he got to see more of the proverbial big picture much sooner every time they spoke, and he looked forward to a lifetime of discovery as her friend.

"So, you want to meet Katie's dad too?" John said.

"Of course!" Mac laughed. "He's a 501c3, and you know how much I love not-for-profit corporations!"

There was something especially fascinating about Mac when she was on a mission. John loved to watch her gear up and go. Whether it was one of their Parkour runs, tracking down a suitable employee for a client, or, in this case, "getting rid of" six point four million dollars, Mac's ability to focus on a task was inspiring.

Filling Empty Houses, Inc. used donated office space in the Miami warehouse district. Ted Conners owned Ted's Beds, and appeared in his own television and radio commercials as "The Sultan of Snooze." There was an oversized cardboard cut-out of the "Sultan" just inside the mattress warehouse, and Mac made John stand beside it while she snapped a picture with her cell phone.

"The camera always adds 20 pounds or so," said the very short man walking towards them across the concrete floor.

"And apparently a couple of vertical feet as well," Mac laughed. "I'm Mac, and this is John. Benny Lopez said we could find him here."

"Right this way," Ted said, pointing down one of the floor-to-ceiling rows of mattresses, "Their entrance is actually in back, but I'll walk you through to his office from here. Need a mattress by any chance?"

"He does," Mac said, pointing a thumb at John, who

suddenly had a new best friend.

"Benny's a bit on the crazy side," Ted said as they walked. "Maybe that's why I like him so much. He loves helping people who need help, but he doesn't just put a roof over their heads, he makes them work hard for their roof, and then he makes them pass it on by helping the next family, and the next. Look at this."

Ted opened a door into the rear loading area. There were three shipping and receiving bays, but one had been transformed into a carless car wash and a rehab clinic for used mattresses. There were people doing spot removal, a lady was hand stitching rips, another was tying in new springs, two men wearing brightly colored Crocs ran steamer machines over mattresses like they were mowing bouncy lawns, and against the back wall, two teenagers were deconstructing mattresses too far gone to restore, and salvaging good springs, foam, and other parts which could be used to salvage other mattresses.

"I take them in on trade, so-to-speak," Ted said. "Nobody likes to haul mattresses, and my guys do it every day, but then I always had to pay to trash the old ones. When Benny's clients are done in here, the recycled mattresses are like new, and the junk I do have to have hauled off is reduced by 60%. Gotta love it!"

Benny's office was painted with paint cans. Every inch of wall space was stacked, floor-to-ceiling with donated cans of paint from every company John and Mac had ever heard of, as well as a host of Spanish labeled cans, obviously manufactured elsewhere. Here and there the stacks had been fashioned into makeshift shelf units and were lined with three ring binders. Benny rose from an ancient military surplus metal desk when Ted led them in, and everybody got acquainted. Ted made to excuse himself, but John interrupted him, and asked if he'd mind hanging around for a few minutes. He winked at Mac, and she went into her spiel.

"We don't want to re-invent the wheel, Benny," she said, "and you've driven a long ways down this road, so we're asking for your help. We've just created a not-for-profit corporation called Personal Space, Inc., we think our two endeavors would dovetail nicely, and we know that if you're willing to help us, more of our resources will go where they're needed much sooner. And you," she said, turning to Ted Connors, "let's just say that we didn't stumble in your front door by accident. We'd like both of you to serve on our board."

Mac was brilliant, and John watched in amazement as she roped the two men in so smoothly and so effortlessly, he wondered whether they might later look back on this moment and think it had all been their idea. Benny Lopez put families in the same kind of homes Mac squatted in, and the City of Miami and its police department had already agreed that it was not their problem unless a bank or a financing corporation stepped forward to raise a stink about how their unsellable property had been repaired, repainted, re-landscaped, and otherwise had its inherent value greatly increased...at no expense to themselves. So far, none of them had. And every family moved in knowing that, at some point, they might be required to leave. None of them cared either, because the community Benny Lopez had created, would help them again if they were not yet ready to take on rent payments on their own.

Personal Space, Inc. would help Benny's efforts on many levels, but Mac had put her perceptive finger right on John's fuzzy dream, and now his design work and Mac's new-found money would help create private shelter for individuals, who, for whatever reasons, never fit into families, communities, church groups, etc. They couldn't help everybody, and they couldn't help individuals with mental health issues directly—perhaps, in time, they would find others who would—but what they were determined to do was to provide a safe, private sanctuary, a place to retreat to when everything else about life proved too overwhelming. At least that was the plan.

## Chapter 30: Room and Board

It was the access to her own laundered cash flow that finally pushed her over the edge, and as agreeable as Mac had eventually become with Oscar Wright's suggestion about creating a 501c3 corporation rather than giving the enigmatic fortune to some random charity in order to separate herself from it as quickly as possible, and as much as she enjoyed seeing John's vision come to life, she did not enjoy all the responsibilities that came with running a not-for-profit. There was nothing "off the grid" about it, and while Oscar, with the help of his accountant, Fred Hoover, handled all the legal applications, all the quarterly reports to the IRS, and even agreed to sit on the board of directors, she was the president. She felt like an Amway sales associate who had to target family and friends in order to make their quota, but she eventually seated the board, hired a small office staff, and very quickly learned to delegate responsibility.

In retrospect, making John choose the last three board

members might not have been the best idea she ever had, but it certainly proved interesting. Dan Stone and Grandmother Renee Persons had both agreed hesitantly. While John was away at school they had bonded like a mother and a long lost prodigal son. Dan checked in on her often, and couldn't do enough for the old woman, and Grandmother Renee suddenly had an audience that didn't walk out confused in the middle of her sage offerings of advice. They cooked together, watched NCIS on TV religiously together, and, to John's credit, were soon equally enthusiastic about Personal Space, Inc.

John also tapped Abraham Jacobs for the board of directors, and, trying on a little of the finesse he admired so much in Mac, convinced the right wing capitalist that a public image of concern for those who were struggling to survive in Miami was not only good for business, but would afford his company free advertisement when the technologies he and John would develop together found their crossover niche in the real world.

"It never crossed over for Kisho Kurokawa," Abraham had argued. "What makes you think it will cross over now?"

"The timing was all wrong back then," John answered. "Kurokawa was a great architect, and way ahead of his time. His 'plug-in' capsule designs are still heavily used in hotels for Japanese commuters, but the rest of the world was looking to the American 'McMansion' model. Being seen as successful was all about having way more space than you and your family could ever really use...except *maybe* at Christmas, but even that was a pathetic rationale. Times have changed, boss, and America is already beginning to lead the way in the downsizing of everything."

"Miami is booming," Abraham said.

"Miami *appears* to be doing somewhat better," John corrected him, "because so many young professionals have been drawn here of late, but nobody's talking about how many of them give up and move away once they realize how expensive it is to live here. Not to mention the crisis everyone *is* talking about...affordable housing for all of the minimum, and below minimum, wage service workers needed to keep a vacation destination running. Used to be that 'migrant camps' were for produce and cotton pickers, but there are houses all over south Florida with wall-to-wall and floor-to-ceiling beds for service workers who send nearly every dollar they make home to foreign countries."

"There is that," Abraham conceded.

"And the vacation industry's own studies show a dramatic drop in high end destination stays, and an increase in stays at the little 1950's style motels and condos from Jacksonville to Key West on the east coast, and from Pensacola to Naples on the Gulf. Given a choice between a huge $600 a night hotel room with a 40" flat screen TV that leaves them no money to be a tourist with, or a 350 square foot efficiency condo in the middle Keys for $600 a *week*, where both Key West and Miami are an hour and a half drive away, folks are already voting with their wallets. Even hostels are becoming all the rage. The jobs aren't all coming back, ever. The unions are in shambles, and the jobs that do become available will have to be more competitive with global averages. America is downsizing, boss. It has to. Are we going to lead the way, or hope to catch up once everyone else is already there?"

"OK, boy wonder," Abraham laughed, "let's see what you've got."

There was nothing about having a checkbook that appealed to Mac. She had become very comfortable being, quite possibly, the only professional left in America without a checking account or an ATM card. So, after quizzing Oscar about his buddy, Fred Hoover, she made the kindly accountant Private Space's controller. She thought it a brilliant executive decision...until the phone calls began coming on a daily basis. As John and Abraham moved from drawing blueprints to building a prototype, the number of purchase orders went from trickling across

Fred Hoover's desk to a steady stream, most of them for items the poor man had never heard of.

"I have a P.O. here for a 7051-684B Star-Tel motherboard controller unit, Mac," Fred would call up and say, his discomfort level apparent even over the phone. "I have no idea what that is, or what it's for."

"Neither do I, Fred," Mac always answered as calmly as she could. "Who signed the P.O.?"

"Well, Mr. Ghostwalker did, but...."

"Then it's fine, Fred. I like to think of it all as Lego blocks. They're building a high tech little Lego house, so whenever you see those purchase orders, just substitute red Lego or blue Lego in your head and send out the check, OK?"

"Well, OK, Mac."

"God bless him, he means well," Mac said to John as they snuck in a short Parkour run, "he'd rather you cut off his finger than catch him writing a check for something unnecessary, but he's going to put me back in the psych ward. How's the model coming along?"

"Really well," John said. "We're going to have to get bids on all the toys, but the basic unit is remarkably cheap to build, and linking them up won't be as bad as I thought. It turns out Abraham is something of a NASA geek, so he figured that out right away. He wants to call it a 'Space Station.' What do you think?"

"That's much better than the 'capsule' or 'pod' names you were telling me about. How many could you link together?"

"As many as you wanted," but beyond four wouldn't really be cost effective, or to the point, but somebody's bound to do it just for the novelty if this thing ever crosses over. How are you, by the way? You look pretty wasted."

"I haven't been sleeping well lately."

"Me either," John said as they wearily climbed the fire escape stairway. "Maybe it's the smoke from all those fires in the Everglades."

## Chapter 31: Space Station Miami

The Space Station prototype debuted on a Miami news broadcast, but the network picked up the story, and within a week reporters and science writers from across the globe were descending on south Florida. Billed as a "high tech solution to the high cost of living" by a particularly enthusiastic tech writer, the phrase caught on, and before one homeless person ever thought about seeking refuge in one, potential buyers were lining up for a test drive...and once they got their turn inside the Space Station, it was next to impossible to get them out.

Gone was any resemblance to a coffin. Sitting there on a slightly modified boat trailer, John's take on Kisho Kurokawa's capsule looked more like the space shuttle. It was ten feet long, and four foot up and down. Inside, there was a round, one-way privacy "port" window in the platform bed's headboard at the front of the "ship," and an almost invisible "hatch" with a louvered window at the rear. The tilt-down HDTV mounted into the ceiling also served as a computer screen and a security monitor, and the swiveling "command chair" in a small foyer called the "command center" functioned as desk chair, dinner table chair, and a *Millennium Falcon*-like gunner's seat when playing video games. This last certainly didn't help shorten the waiting line to come aboard for a tour.

Along the "starboard side," there was a row of small appliances that somehow looked way cooler than they did in their more typical surroundings, the iconic American recreational vehicle. On the port side, just inside the hatch, the tiny bathroom was sit-down only, but the faucet in the tiny sink doubled as a retractable shower nozzle and the floor drained just like any shower enclosure. The built-in Dolby surround system in the main cabin could "dock" any mp3 player, and from a "home theater" perspective gave new meaning to feeling like you were "in" the movie. One of Mac's favorite features was the L.E.D. "mood lighting" feature, and when combined with an extensive onboard selection of nature sounds, even the most hardcore insomniac would be hard pressed to remain awake. Media types were offering John and Abraham obscene amounts of money just to spend one night "on board," and Abraham, at least, was happy to accommodate them.

"My God, John," Abraham exclaimed after tucking in yet another journalist for the night, "you were right! They're crazy about this thing!"

The blush was fading some for John and Mac. "What do you mean 'he's taking orders?'" Mac said. "We haven't figured out how to produce them yet."

"I know," John said, "but Abraham probably won't sleep until he nails that down too. He just formed a new company, with four owners, called Space Station, LLC, and you and I will get our ownership papers tomorrow or the next day."

"Has he forgotten why we did this? How long can we hold our finger in that dike while we try to actually get these to the people who really need them?"

"It's my fault," John said. "I knew why he got involved. Who can blame him? But I had so much fun creating it, and all the micro technology is so damn cheap right now. I just got a little carried away, and I certainly underestimated the cool factor."

"We can still make this work," Mac said. "What do you suppose would have happened if Apple had told everybody who wanted an iPod or an iPad on Day One that they couldn't get in line unless they gave five bucks to the Red Cross?"

"The Red Cross could have bought a butt-load of new blankets."

"Right! And so what if all the Space Station wanna-gets had to pick up a piece of the tab for getting one to a homeless person?"

"Brilliant! You're a genius! Even Abraham will love the press that brings him!"

"So a preacher, a priest, and a rabbi are having a friendly ecumenical discussion," Abraham said to John and Mac over lunch, "and the rabbi explained his take on giving back to God. 'I draw a circle on the ground, stand in it, and throw my week's pay up in the air. Everything that lands outside the circle, I put in the collection plate.' The priest laughed and said 'I do the same thing, only I give the money that falls inside the circle.' The preacher smiled and said 'I don't bother with the circle. After I throw my money up in the air, I keep however much of it God didn't catch.'"

"Actually, it's called tithing," Abraham said after John and Mac had laughed appreciatively. "You give ten percent of your income to God, or in our case, to the homeless. For every one Space Station you purchase, you put up ten percent of getting one for a needy person, knowing that Personal Space, Inc. will match your funds. Then you get a tax deduction...it's perfect! We could even print up stickers of appreciation that you can post on your Station and the one you helped give away."

Abraham got several preliminary quotes on production of the Space Station, but everybody seemed to favor having it built locally, regardless of the cost. The "bid" went to Coral Gables Construction, primarily because they were a known entity, and they set up the factory in Homestead. Bringing over 300 new jobs to the area didn't hurt on the PR front, and they wasted no time turning the spotlight into more publicity and more orders.

On John's recommendation, Mac assigned Dan Stone the title "Director of Housing," gave him an adequate salary, and put him to work drawing up rules and screening homeless and indigent applicants. Since Grandmother Renee had de-toxed him on her own organic herbal tea and then gotten him into the AA group that met at the local Catholic church, Dan was a new man. He shadowed Benny Lopez, and learned everything the old hand had to teach him. As the first Space Stations became available, Dan put his memories of boot camp to good use, and was extremely convincing when it came to laying down the law. "You screw up with the law, you're back on the street. You damage the goods, you're back on the street. You don't show up for work, you're back on the street."

Dan found a job for every applicant, regardless of health, age, or disability; there was always something they could do for either Personal Space, Inc. or Filling Empty Houses, Inc., even if it was as simple as stuffing envelopes. If they wanted to work for a charity of their own choosing, that was cool too, but everybody passed it forward somewhere. They called him "Dan the Man," and it soon became apparent to everyone at Personal Space, Inc. that the people he reached out to would follow him anywhere.

Dan and John put their heads together when it came to placing the Space Station units, both understanding the need for privacy. Finding out-of-the-way nooks and crannies was second nature to both of them, and they figured out very quickly how to hide a Space Station in plain sight, and because they could attach a unit to a commercial building or a warehouse without giving the user access to those businesses, getting business owners to donate the space they weren't using, along with a negligible amount of electricity, water, and sewer access became much easier. Business owners were legitimately concerned about the "mess" that generally defined any space occupied by the homeless, but if there wasn't already a hedge present at a potential site, Personal Space, Inc. volunteers would plant one, and when Dan the Man explained that cleanliness was next to Godliness, and that the unclean would soon be "back on the street," both his sponsors and his clients became true believers.

## Chapter 32: Lost and Found

"Professor! It's me, Maria. You gots to come out!"

The knocking was insistent, but Elana Gomez clutched her stash of books, rocked in place, and sung to herself in a voice so soft no one would hear it, ever.

"You know me," Maria whispered loudly as she continued to knock on the wooden shipping crate. "I wouldn't bother you unless it was important."

Dan Stone stood quietly next to a pile of old pallets and the wooden crate that had the word "Quickie" stamped on it in numerous places. Maria Warren had begged him to come with her to the chain link enclosed parking lot behind South Miami Medical Supply Company. The industrial park where the company did business bordered one of the poorest neighborhoods in Miami, infamous for swallowing up bewildered tourists who, thinking they were on their way to the Florida Keys, had badly misjudged the travel time from the Georgia border and compounded their weary misery by missing the Homestead Extension Exit that was, in fact, how one remained on the Florida Turnpike going south. By mistakenly following the main thoroughfare, they had, instead, been channeled first onto Interstate 95, right through the heart of Miami, and then been dumped unceremoniously onto busy US 1 where the stoplights halted them every other block or so.

"I have a man here with me, Professor, a good man," Maria went on. "He can help you find a clean, safe, quiet place to live. He was in the Army, like your son, and now he helps people like us. I read about him in the paper and I brought him here to meet you."

Maria Gomez was a first for Dan. Clearly as destitute as any of the other homeless people he had interviewed, and as cunning and street savvy as they came, but instead of making her case when her turn finally came, she had pleaded the case of Elana Gomez. "She is very smart, even has a Master's degree," Maria had told him, "and she used to teach us at the community center, but she had a breakdown or a relapse or something when her son died in Afghanistan. She has what's called Asperger syndrome, and Elana says that a lot of homeless people have undiagnosed cases, but it can be managed." So Dan called Benny Lopez, who verified what Maria said about Asperger syndrome, and now here he was trying to coax a depressed and terrified woman out of one box and into a better one.

"Elana?" he said quietly, urging Maria to stop knocking and step out of the way. "My name is Dan Stone, and I'm sorry if we're scaring you, but your friend, Maria, is very worried about you. She tells me that you've helped a lot of homeless people understand why they get so afraid sometimes, and now she wants me to help you. No one is going to touch you, or make you do anything you don't want to do, but I'd like to give you some things to read. One is a newspaper article about what we do. It's even got my picture in it so you can see that I'm who I say I am. The other thing I want to give you is a brochure about the new housing units we're setting up for people who need them. Can I pass these things to you through the crack here?" Dan said, holding the materials up in front of him, hoping that the woman was peeking out.

Dan and Maria waited breathlessly for some indication that Elana was even in the shipping crate. For a moment nothing happened, but then the wooden box tipped backwards slightly, and a slender hand slipped out from underneath, palm up. Dan gently placed the papers in Elana's hand and stepped away. "Thank you," Dan said. "Take your time reading that, and I'll check back with you."

Maria said that Elana's son had worked here as a wheelchair technician before his Reserve unit was called up, and so the owners overlooked his mom's trespassing. They'd even gone so far as to leave bags of food and water next to the crate from time to time, renting a porta-john for the parking lot, and instructing the trash guys to leave the wooden box completely alone. That was a good sign. Dan knocked on the shipping and receiving door and then went in to pitch the owners about setting up a Space Station next to the building.

His next move was a call to Grandmother Renee. If anyone could talk Elana Gomez out of her electric wheelchair shipping crate it was the honorary president of Personal Space, Inc. and the honorary grandmother of everyone who knew her.

"Are you up for a field trip, Grandmother?" he said when she answered her phone. "I have a very frightened lady over here in Miami who could really use a grandmother right now."

"You just come get me, child, and we'll see what we can do."

It took several days to get the Space Station installed behind the medical supply store and a decorative hedge planted to camouflage it, but Grandmother Renee spent a few hours on each of those days sitting in a folding chair under the live oaks, talking to Elana Gomez through the slats in her box.

For the first day, Grandmother Renee just talked quietly to the woman, as if nothing was out of the ordinary. "Hello, Elana? My name is Renee Persons, and I work with the organization that puts folks into the little apartments like our Daniel is setting up for you out here. It sure was nice of the folks at the store to let him do this for you. They tell me that your son, David, was a fine young man, and that he loved you very much. I was never able to have children myself, and after my husband died in World War II, well, I just started treating everyone like my children. I'm a Miccosukee Indian, dear, and I live out off Tamiami Trail near the edge of the Reservation."

Calm and comfort just flowed with Grandmother Renee's words, and when it was time for Dan to drive her home, she acted just like she'd been over to Elana's house for tea. "Well, I'd better head home now, Elena, but thank you for letting me come over, and if you don't mind, dear, I believe I'll stop by tomorrow and see how you're doing. Have a good night now."

When Dan picked her up the next day, she took along a Thermos and two ancient tea cups and saucers. "Good day to you, Elana," she said as she settled into her lawn chair. "I brought you a bit of my herbal tea. Here, tip that back for me, would you, dear?"

The crate tipped back on command, and Elana reached out and took the proffered teacup. "Oh, my!" whispered Elana Gomez seconds later. "Miss Renee, why this is just delightful, and so fresh. Thank you so very much!"

"Well, dear," Grandmother Renee said with a wink over at Dan Stone, "you are most welcome."

They both sipped in silence for a few moments before Grandmother Renee took another risk. "I was wondering, dear, if I could persuade you to tell me a little about David. I should like very much to know more about him."

For the next two hours, through tears, laughter, and several more cups of tea, Elana whispered her son's story to her new Native American friend. After being raped while a patient in the mental health wing of a Miami area hospital, Elana, with the help of her aging mother, had decided to keep the child. Her mother passed when the boy was twelve, but Elana not only continued raising David by herself, but acquired an undergraduate degree and a Masters degree in Psychology from the University of Miami while doing so. Elana had faced her Asperger syndrome diagnosis head on, learning everything she could about it, and—often with David in tow—had helped set up support groups throughout the state. Grandmother Renee made a mental note to let that "tribe" know that one of their own was now in need. Elana was teaching at the Miami-Dade County Community College when David joined the Army Reserves, and both of their lives seemed stable at last. Then, less than a year later, one knock on her apartment door had changed everything.

"It's coming along quite nicely, dear," Grandmother Renee said on the third day. "Here, I had Daniel take some pictures for you. " She slipped Dan's cell phone under the lip of the crate. "Just push the button with the arrow pointing right to see the next picture when you're ready. You know, child, it will be very safe in your new home, and no one can come in unless you want them to."

"I am so ashamed," Elana whispered as she looked at the photos. "I thought I was past all this."

"Well, you were, dear," Grandmother Renee said, "and there's nothing to be ashamed of. You helped others get past it too, but there are no rules about how many times life can knock a person backwards. That's why we always have to keep focused on moving forward as best we can today. Yesterday's gone, and it doesn't count for anything anymore. We just have today."

"Thank you, Miss Renee. You are very kind. Do you think you could walk with me if I were to go over there and have a closer look?"

"I'd love nothing more, dear. You just say the word when you're ready and I'll have Daniel give us a tour. I've never actually been inside one myself, so perhaps you could tell me what it's like in there. It does appear rather cozy, don't you think?"

"Well, yes I do, and I'm particularly curious about the colored lighting and the mood music. These things have proven very therapeutic for persons with Asperger syndrome. We tend to get over stimulated, especially in crowed places, but soft lights and calming music can be very helpful."

"Well, Elana, John Ghostwalker invented these little apartments, and he built those lights and sound effects into them because he doesn't always like crowded places much either, so there you go!"

And there they went, arm-in-arm, strolling across the gravel back lot and slipping sideways through the narrow opening in the new hedge.

"What's this?" Elana whispered to Dan.

"We made you a little space for a garden. Maria told us you used to grow your own herbs."

"Oh my," she said to Grandmother Renee, "he is very nice, isn't he?"

"Yes he is, dear. Well, here we are. In you go!"

Elena stepped up into her new home, sat down in the command chair, and turned in slow circles. "It's wonderful," she said. "How can I ever repay you?"

"Well, dear," Grandmother Renee said as she peered in through the open hatch, "when you're settled in and feeling better, you could teach us more about how to help other folks with issues like yours. How would that be?"

"I would like that, Miss Renee. I would like that very much."

– The Ghostwalker File –

# Chapter 33: Repercussions

Benny the Crutch was in his glory, headed south on the I-95 corridor with the sun shining and the top down. He hadn't been to Florida in years, and one of the reasons he'd restored the old Cadillac ragtop in the first place was his determination to retire to Miami. Benny figured he was getting close, especially because the boss had a soft spot for him in his heart, and could hardly deny an early retirement to the faithful soldier who took a bullet in the leg for him. Truth be told, Benny hated guns, and though he still carried the old Smith & Wesson .38 in the glove box, he hadn't fired it since that fateful day when he shot himself in the leg. It was an ugly scene, bullets flying wildly during a sloppy Baltimore turf dispute in the early 80's, but Benny never quite understood why everyone thought he'd caught a bullet aimed at the boss. Regardless, that misconception made his career as a good fellow and a trusted lieutenant. Even though the boys sometimes ragged him about his choices in shirt colors, his black aluminum Canadian crutch became a constant reminder to friends and foes alike that Benny was a man willing to die for the cause ... even though he still had nightmares about his first and only gun fight and was thinking way more about finding cover than he was about protecting the boss that day.

His bum right leg gave him more trouble with each passing winter, and from what he'd heard, Florida was the place to go if you had arthritis related aches and pains. He used his crutch to operate the gas, and kept his left toe resting lightly on the brake as he passed the first "Pedro says" sign for the famous South of the Border tourist complex. He was fifty miles from the North Carolina/South Carolina line. As a kid, he'd always wanted to stop at South of the Border, but his dad was always on a schedule, and basically thought anything aimed that brazenly at tourists was best avoided. Benny had a real Havana cigar glowing between the fingers of his right hand, lots of money in his pocket, and his dad had long since gone to his reward, so tonight Benny was going to be a bone fide tourist, trap or no.

Pedro's Motor Lodge was something of a letdown. He wasn't sure what he'd expected, but aside from some furniture upgrades, Benny was pretty sure that his room in the concrete block bunker-like building with its tiny A&W style overhung parking places hadn't changed much since he'd futilely begged his dad to stop there in 1965. The same could be said for Pedro's Diner where he ordered his breakfast the next morning, but he was a basic eggs and bacon kind of guy, and aside from the complimentary grits, it suited him just fine. North Carolina always seemed iffy to him, but South Carolina was committed. Benny was in the South, and as the miles flew by, he just pictured himself in Florida for good. He was almost through Georgia when his cell phone rang.

"Shit," he said as he locked his right elbow into the crutch sleeve and eased off the hand grip with his palm so he could pass the cigar off to his left hand while he steered with his left elbow. Keeping the pressure on the gas, Benny leaned the crutch towards his chest and used his cigar fingers to fish around in the pocket of his new Tommy Bahama shirt for his cell. "Who the fuck is this, and what the fuck do you want?" he yelled into the phone when he'd finally managed to get it near his ear.

"Who the fuck do you think it is?"

"Oh, sorry boss! What do you need?"

"A little change in plans, Benny. Miami called to say that the Feds are watching them a little too closely right now, so the meeting's being moved to a more secure location. I'm texting you the directions."

"OK, boss. You think they're gonna go for this? Once I tell them about the girl and her company, they don't need our help to put the squeeze on her."

"You just gotta sell it, Benny. We're doin' all the dirty work for them, and then once we get our money back, the cash cow's all theirs, free and clear."

"And if they say no, I burn the factory and grab the girl."

"Well, I've been thinking about that, Benny. The fire we can pass off as an accident, but if we snatch the girl, Miami knows it was us and we don't look so good to the family. It's all about respect, right Benny?"

"If you say so, boss."

"I say so. Carry on!"

The phone went dead. "Carry on?" Benny muttered as he fumbled the phone back into his flowery pocket. "What the fuck is that shit?"

Over lunch in a Jacksonville barbeque joint, Benny read the texted directions and wrote them out on a napkin because there was no real address to plug into his GPS, just a bunch of turns with a gravel parking lot at the end. A few sunny hours later, he exited Interstate 95 at the Jupiter Exit and got on the Florida Turnpike as instructed. He never relished the idea of hauling the McKnight kid back to Baltimore in his trunk, mostly because he wasn't at all certain how far her crazy old man intended to go when it came time for her to "pay for this." What had the kid ever done except run away from the bastard? Who wouldn't?

Benny almost missed the Okeechobee Road Exit, but

cut back over from the passing lane with inches to spare, and by the time he swung south on Route 997, he was beginning to feel a little edgy. Meeting a mob boss in Miami was one thing, but now there was nothing on his right but Everglades swamp. Miles of it. He passed the occasional nursery farm, but otherwise he was just too far out in the boonies. Sure, Maryland had some boonies, even wet ones, but you didn't see hungry alligators every few hundred yards up north. And the idea that someone had built a casino out in that soggy wasteland was seeming more improbable to him by the mile, but just as he was about to pull over and call the boss, he saw it. There it was, the Miccosukee Resort & Casino, sitting on the northwest corner of the first major intersection he'd seen since leaving the turnpike. The signs said that 997 was also Krome Avenue, and the napkin said to turn right onto Route 41 at the casino, so he did.

He clocked the next two miles and watched for the gravel parking lot, and there, ahead on his right, was a long black limousine parked in the lot of an old fish camp. "Shit," Benny said to himself, "could you be any more conspicuous? Helluva way to give the Feds the slip." As he pulled up behind the limo, a uniformed driver got out and opened one of the rear doors. Benny was shifting into Park as a tall skinny man stepped out and began walking towards him in a bright chartreuse tuxedo that seemed to sparkle as he walked.

"Daniel!" the man shouted back at his driver, "Please get this thirsty gentleman a cold beer at once."

The driver nodded and proceeded to pop the limo's trunk and dig around in a blue plastic cooler while the skinny man turned back to Benny as he walked around to the passenger door of the drop-top Caddy. "Hello there! You must be Mr. B. Crutch. I'm Louis, and I must say that your car is simply fabulous!" With an all-too-graceful Vanna White sweep of his backhand toward the white leather passenger seat, he said: "May I?"

Before Benny could answer, Louis seemed to float over the passenger door and drop lightly into the bucket seat where he actually giggled as he clapped his hands in front of him like a school girl. "Marvelous! You've restored it to perfection Mr. Crutch, and I can't wait to go for a joy ride with you!"

Benny was about to tell the man that there was no way in hell there was going to be any fucking joy riding when a silver serving tray appeared in front of him with an ice cold can of his favorite beer on it. He reached for it instinctively, thinking perhaps he could hold his tongue just long enough to enjoy a few refreshing swallows.

"Thank you, dear Daniel. That will be all," said the sparkly man as he swished his driver away with the back of his fingers. "We want to be alone now."

Benny was pretty sure that he did not want to be alone with this bizarre mob boss, and his mind swirled around in awe at how different things were down south. He'd never met the man before, but Louis Corbieri was notoriously tough, and rumors had it that his crew would do anything for him. Sure, Miami was a gay-friendly place, but this just wasn't right. Benny tried to calm himself with another swig of cold beer.

"You must be thirsty after that long, long drive," Louis said, "but time is money, so we'd better get down to business."

"Yes, sir, Mr. Corbieri," Benny managed between gulps, glad to see things heading back on track.

"Now let me assure you, Mr. Crutch, that I will do things to you that will rock your world and leave you begging for more, but I must insist on payment up front. Business is business."

Benny's right hand shot toward the glove box so fast it made him dizzy, but the sparkling slender man was faster.

"There, there now, my sexy little big man, you won't be needing that. Try to relax and go with it." Benny tried unsuccessfully to focus on his right hand, saw Louis bend up his blurry looking wrist and apply pressure to his thumb joint, and felt himself completely immobilized. Then, from a long way off, Benny thought he heard himself say: "Oh fuck."

## Chapter 34: Up the Tree Without a Paddle

Benny the Crutch woke up in a tree. Well, several trees, to be more accurate. They all sort of grew together, and below him, their roots stood interlinked like dozens of those four-footed canes he had used during his physical therapy days at the hospital. The roots created a stilt island, and water flowed slowly but steadily beneath them, sparkling brilliantly where the early morning sun shot though. He was sprawled out, facing the ground, across a tangle of branches about seven or eight feet off the unusual ground. As his eyes came more into focus, Benny saw his Canadian crutch lying across the root knees near the island's eastern edge, but it seemed to sparkle even more than the water. It became obvious within moments that someone had coated his black crutch with glue and then sprinkled it liberally with multi-colored glitter.

His head pounded, the skin on his face felt dry and tight, and his lips were greasy. Benny wiped at them and nearly fell from his precarious perch when he saw the bright red lipstick transfer on the back of his hand. "Someone has to pay for this," he said to no one in particular as he reached slowly for his shirt pocket. But there was no shirt pocket. His new floral colored Tommy Bahama shirt had been replaced with a pink plunging ruffled silk blouse. No pocket, no cell phone, and no one coming to help. A string of red plastic beads hung loose around his neck, and the morning breeze he felt between his legs suggested that he wasn't wearing his slacks anymore.

Just a few yards out from his crutch, two sets of beady eyes stared up at him hungrily. Had he not seen so many gators driving down, they might have passed for a couple of mostly submerged logs. Benny tried shifting his weight a little, and felt one of his shoes catch on a branch and pull free. The red leather pump that dropped onto the roots below him didn't help his sense of angry desperation. That's when he heard someone whistling "She'll be Coming 'Round the Mountain," and saw the alligators disappear in a swirling disturbance of Everglades swamp water. A camouflage colored canoe glided up to his island, and the gay guy's driver stopped whistling and stepped lightly onto the island, still decked out in his well-pressed uniform.

"I have a special delivery for a Mr. Benny Crutch," he said to no one in particular. "Mr. Crutch?"

"Fuck you!" Benny said, regretting it immediately. "I mean, here. I'm up here."

"Why, so you are," said the driver, who glanced up and walked directly towards Benny's perch. "I'm to give you this, and await your response." The man promptly returned to the canoe, pulled a Kindle reader out from under his seat, and began reading as if nothing whatsoever was out of the ordinary.

Benny opened the 9" X 12" envelope and scanned the 8" X 10" glossies of his previous evening's adventures. Between the dark glasses and the creative poses, no one would ever believe he'd been unconscious though it all. "Bedtime with fuckin' Bernie," he said to himself.

"Wouldn't you know it?" The letter was straightforward:

*Dear Benny. You've got a couple choices here. First, you can dismiss my driver and work your way out of your present predicament as best you can. While you're attempting to do that, copies of the enclosed photos will be delivered to your boss in Baltimore and to the real Louis Corbieri here in Miami. That probably won't do much for your reputation as a tough guy, or for your current retirement plans, but hey, they're your family, right? They'll understand.*

*On the other hand, you can ask Daniel to escort you back to your beautiful newly painted Cadillac and follow the directions I've left on your dashboard to the FBI offices in Tampa. Agent Taylor Maine will take your statement, and if you're convincing enough, he assures me that you can retire to a sunny little southern bungalow all your own. If, however, Agent Maine hasn't seen your gorgeous face by the day after tomorrow, you get to party with me again, and believe me, it won't be as much fun the next time.*

*One more thing. If you choose Plan B, check yourself out in the enclosed mirror before you decide to get creative with my driver. There's a good fellow!*

There was, in fact, a small mirror in the bottom of the envelope, and aside from the gaudy make-up Benny saw smeared all over his face and his eyebrows, there was a tiny red laser dot dancing a little circular jig in the middle of his forehead.

"It just keeps getting better," Benny sighed to himself as he returned everything to the envelope. "Hey Daniel," he said as politely as he could, "would you mind handing me my crutch? I've got an appointment in Tampa, and I've just got to get out of these clothes if I want to make a good fucking first impression."

Two days later, on a conference call between Baltimore and Miami, Dan Stone and Seth Lowenstein filled everyone in on their caper. Seth admitted that he'd been wiretapping the Baltimore mob ever since the reading of Sarah's will, and Dan just kept laughing and saying how fun it was to play his part as the driver. Several of Dan's homeless Space Station tenants had helped Nathan Blackfeather repaint Benny's Caddy overnight at the Macco shop in Homestead. That really had been a great party, and they all agreed that the now pink car with its "Save the Boobies" pin-striping would definitely help Benny hide in plain sight as he began his new life in Witness Protection.

"Mr. Crutch checked in with my FBI friend in Tampa," Seth said, "and he sang like a canary. Agent Maine said that he seemed especially enthusiastic when it came to conversations about your dad, Mac. I guess he didn't like him very much."

"Nobody does," Mac said. "Will dear daddy do prison time?"

"Almost certainly...at least eventually, when the investigation is complete."

"Then all's well that ends well."

## Chapter 35: An Ah-Ha Moment

Sergeant Lester "Tubby" Roundtree had been summoned. Very few tribe members refused such a summons, and as he cleaned up the front desk at the tribal police station for the next shift, he couldn't help thinking about how far he'd come from his misguided youth, and how much of the credit for that must be accorded to his summoner. From as far back as he could remember, Tubby dwarfed everyone else his age, and it wasn't too long before he was bigger than everyone he knew. As he came into his teens, Miami was becoming known as a Mecca for rap and hip-hop music. Related events became annual affairs in South Beach, and Tubby noticed very quickly that large men seemed to be readily accepted if they could "busta rhyme." Certainly seeing these guys proudly going shirtless in their videos, while surrounded by adoring bikini-clad young women, had more than a subtle effect on his self-image and his aspirations. Sadly though, Tubby had little or no rhythm, even less ability to carry a tune, and his poetry affected people in most unfortunate ways.

That so much hope could be dashed so quickly and so cruelly was a teenager's worst nightmare, and when Tubby crashed, he crashed big. In the midst of his deepest, darkest, most unfathomable despair, when his parents, his teachers, and his friends all failed to break through, Tubby Roundtree received his first summons. He didn't want to go, he certainly didn't feel like going anywhere, but as far as he could tell, no one in the tribe had ever said "no" to Grandmother Renee. And why on earth she wanted a fence, of all things, and why she had insisted that he help her build it, Tubby had no clue. He just gathered up his anger and despair and took it all to Grandmother Renee's little cottage, where together, they memorialized it in the form of a white picket fence. Such was the irresistible power of her love.

The drive from the police station took less than five minutes.

"Lester? Is that you child? Come in, come in!"

"Yes, Grandmother," he said, "don't get up." He engulfed her gently in his arms, snuck a Milky Way onto her TV tray table, and sat cross-legged at her feet. "What can I do for you, Grandmother?"

"Well, yes, I do have a favor to ask," she said, "but first you must tell me about my children. "

One reason there were very few secrets in the tribe had to do with Grandmother Renee's uncanny ability to interrogate her children. None of them ever realized they were being interrogated; in fact, at the time, they all felt like they were in complete control of themselves and their own personal sense of discretion. It was only afterwards that they often found themselves somewhat chagrinned by their own frankness about certain delicate matters. But in the end, everyone knew that Grandmother Renee loved all her children, and that regardless of how much or how little trouble they might be mixed up with, that love knew no bounds.

So Tubby filled her in on the week's police blotter news: who'd been arrested, who'd been promoted, and who got caught making out behind the Trading Post Gas & Go on Saturday night.

"And your lady friend, Christine, at the crime lab?" Grandmother Renee offered as Tubby wound down. "Is that going well?"

"Well, yes, I think it is," Tubby said. "I did what you said, and asked Christine to take line dancing lessons with me. Turns out neither one of us will ever end up on Dancing with the Stars, but we've survived two lessons, and always have fun."

"That's wonderful to hear, and you tell her I said hello when you give her this for me." She handed Tubby a small brown paper bag. "Go ahead and look inside."

Tubby unrolled the top and looked inside. Two zip-lock baggies, one marked with an "A" and the other marked "B," sat side-by-side. Both appeared to be empty. "Are they empty, Grandmother?"

"No, Child. Each contains several human hairs."

"And you want me to give these to Christine?"

"Yes I do. I want her to run a DNA profile on them," she said matter-of-factly.

Tubby had to pause a second on that one. Grandmother Renee didn't look like she was kidding, she never did, but this was a corker. "So, Grandmother, you want to know who these hairs belong to?"

"Why no, Lester. Don't you think I know who leaves their hair on my furniture?"

"Yes, yes of course you would," Tubby said, irresistibly raising his free hand to his own head of wavy hair. "I just mean what is it you want Christine to test for, exactly?"

"On NCIS, they said that a DNA test can prove whether two people are related. Is that true?"

"Yes, Grandmother, it is true."

"Well then, I'd like Christine to tell me whether person A is related to person B."

"And are you going to tell me who these mysterious people are?"

"Not right now, I don't think," she said, pausing as if lost in thought. "Lester?"

"Yes, Grandmother?"

"Have you ever had an ah-ha moment?"

"A what?"

"Oprah says that an ah-ha moment is when you suddenly see something for the first time…even if it's been right there in front of your nose all along."

"I see," Tubby said, scratching his head and immediately looking to see if any hair fell out. "Like that skinny rapper, calls himself 'Epiphany.' And you've had one of these moments, Grandmother?"

"Yes I have, child. I truly believe I have."

## Chapter 36: Reality Check Please

Edward McKnight was always a control freak, and as long as he had total control (or at least thought he did), he functioned fairly well. Business deals got done, investment decisions were handled competently, and his "public face" was similar enough to that of his ancestors to enable him to maintain his status in the right Baltimore social circles. However, when things didn't go his way, or when he felt slighted or, God forbid, humiliated, Edward slipped into a very dark place. Mental illness comes in all shapes and sizes, and when it comes to psychopathic behavior, Edward McKnight was living proof that while most human beings either live there or they don't, it is actually possible to timeshare.

Sarah McKnight came to this terrible realization about her husband early on in their marriage, and part of her coping/enabling behavior arose from being less afraid of what Edward would do when he checked into the black vacation timeshare than she was of what might happen if he returned "home" to find that his social status and/or financial control of all things had been compromised in some way. So Sarah dutifully managed the "black times" by literally getting Edward to leave Baltimore, and by learning how to hold it all together in his absence. Their southern Colorado lodge in the Sangre de Cristo mountain range was far enough from everything and everyone that a public incident was unlikely, there was more than enough acreage around it so that Edward could shoot a nearly endless supply of wildlife with impunity, and each member of the very highly paid staff, hand-picked and trained by Sarah herself, was a master of containment. What happened on the McKnight mountain estate stayed on the McKnight mountain estate.

Sarah came to understand her husband's business affairs very well during his periodic retreats from sanity, so that by the time Edward made her sign Mac's commitment papers, skimming money from his various mob related deals was relatively easy. Sarah McKnight was a terribly abused woman, and her self-esteem had been battered almost beyond recognition, but she was also extremely intelligent and took passive aggressive payback to dizzying new heights. Unlike Edward, Sarah knew exactly who was really in control. Whatever deal was made, whether it was done by Edward, his father, or his father's father, had forever shackled the McKnights to the Baltimore mob. They were unforgiving masters, and no amount of denial on Edward's part could change the real hierarchy of power. And, in Sarah's case at least, nothing offered freedom from that kind of fear quite like terminal cancer.

Sarah's death set off a complicated chain of events, both in Mac's life, and in Edward's. For Mac, it was a master class in the relentlessly demanding world of resources and responsibility. The jury was still out on how that was going. But for her father, Sarah's death not only revealed, in an instant, the house of worn and tattered cards that was his life, but made it very clear that she, not Edward, had been holding it all together. The collapse began at dinner the very day she passed. Well, that's not exactly true, because there was no dinner. The kitchen staff, having attended to Sarah McKnight with loyalty and compassion throughout her decline, simply walked out of the house that afternoon, right after the nurse notified them that she had called the doctor and that Sarah was gone. Edward sat expectantly at the dining room table for nearly ten minutes that evening before realizing that no one had even set the table. It took him several more moments to figure out that there was no meal forthcoming. He called out for the kitchen staff to no avail.

His driver, Joey Beans, was a mid-level mobster's nephew who lived in the apartment over the garage. He was also being paid to keep an eye out for anything that might not serve the Baltimore mob family's best interests. Joey drove the car around in response to Edward's call.

"Sorry about the Mrs.," Joey said as he held the door. "Where to?"

"That restaurant Sarah likes, down at Scituate Harbor. What's it called?"

"Riva, Sir?"

"Yes, that's it."

"Did you call ahead?"

"I never had to before."

"Yes, well, it's Friday night, Sir, and Mrs. McKnight always called ahead."

"They'll seat me, Joey. Let's go."

Joey closed the door, got behind the wheel, and headed east into town. There was something very cold and disconnected in his boss's eyes, and Joey was a little unnerved. Going out for dinner a couple hours after the coroner's van picks up your dead wife was pretty strange, but then he'd never heard anybody in the Italian mob ever suggested that the Irish were normal. He'd watched the kitchen staff slip out the back door, then the home care nurse left after the coroner arrived, and finally the county meat wagon had taken Mrs. McKnight away. Watching it all from his little apartment was unsettling, but this ride just felt wrong. It had been drilled into him to show deference to Edward McKnight, but neither his uncle nor the real boss seemed to respect the guy. Joey had tried hard to like the man, but it just wasn't happening. On the other hand, he had grown very fond of Sarah.

"This is it," Joey said as he pulled up to the curb and hopped out. The place was packed, and a couple dozen people sat on benches or milled around outside. "Good luck," he said as Edward stepped out and shouldered his way inside. Joey returned to the car and watched to see what would happen. Though he could not hear it, the conversation between his boss and the hostess obviously wasn't going well. Edward's neck got bright red, and as quickly as waiting customers gave him wide berth, the owner swooped in to rescue his hostess. He took Edward's elbow and ushered him outside with no hesitation whatsoever. Joey sprang into action, ran around the car, and stood holding the door for his agitated and shell-shocked boss.

"Mrs. McKnight was a grand lady, may she rest in peace, but you, sir, are no longer welcome here," the restaurant owner said as he manhandled Edward into the backseat much like an arresting police officer might have done with a street thug.

Joey closed the door without a word and pulled away. He held his breath most of the way home.

– Kevin Robinson –

## Chapter 37: High Flying Paranoia

Edward McKnight was, at first, beside himself. But it didn't take long for him to part company with himself altogether. Joey Beans watched it all, up close and personal. By the time Edward returned from the reading of Sarah's secret will with a broken thumb, Joey had taken over at the big house and was virtually indispensable. First he was ordered to prepare meals. Well, more often than not, Joey was warming up meals his Uncle Louie was having sent over from Mamas Rose's restaurant. When the housekeeper never showed up, Joey began changing the sheets and either doing or sending out the laundry too. The money was incredible, as Edward seemed unaware how much cash he shoved into Joey's palm in order to convince himself that he still had some kind of control over his life. But were it not for his uncle's relentless insistence that Joey honor the mob boss's wishes, Joey would have left that night Edward had been tossed out of Riva in front of a sizable audience. The ride home had convinced Joey that

McKnight had crossed over into insanity, and Joey had called his uncle at his very first opportunity.

"He's nuts, Uncle Louie, I mean scary nuts. I want outta here!"

"Joey, I hear you, and I love you like you were my own son—God rest my sister's soul—but the boss is right. Now, more than ever, you gotta stay close to this guy. He might be off his rocker, but he handles a lot of our money, and nothing can happen to him until we know where it all is and how to get it back outta his fancy money washing investment schemes. You hearing me?"

"I do, Uncle Louie, but shit, what do I do if he goes crazy on me?"

"Joey, you're a smart kid, and you grew up hard. McKnight never worked a day in his life. His hands have never been dirt dirty. You can take care of yourself, but he can't. Right now he's got nobody but you, so make him happy and take his money...at least 'til the boss gets ours back. You do that and you'll end up being my boss. How 'bout it?"

"OK, I'll try."

A month later, Joey called his uncle again. "He's been spending hours on his computer, reading newspapers and lotsa magazines like *Architectural Digest* and such, and he said something about me driving him to Florida. Will the boss be OK with that?"

"I'll ask," Uncle Louie said, "but funny you should ask that. You might have just fallen into another job than could move you up. The boss has been talking about sending somebody down there ever since Benny the Crutch went missing. The Miami boss swears Benny never showed up, but who knows? Could be a big opportunity for you."

"OK, whatever," Joey said. "The buzzer's going off. Used to be he buzzed and I brought the car around. Now one buzz is the car, two is he wants me to fix him something to eat, three buzzes is dirty laundry, and so on.

Right now he's just holding the button down. I really gotta go."

Joey found Edward sitting at the dining room table, hunched over a laptop computer, with printouts all around him. There was a large suitcase on the floor next to his chair. Joey couldn't read the print from across the table, but some of the illustrations were of large threaded nuts. Joey thought it seemed fitting somehow.

"What's up, boss? Hungry?"

"No thanks, Joey," Edward said without looking up. "I just ordered up a little surprise for the girl, and so we've got to hit the road if we're going get to Miami before it gets delivered there. Take my bag, pack one for yourself, and bring the car around."

"OK, boss," Joey said. "I'm on it."

Edward McKnight almost never referred to his daughter, Sean, but when he did, he simply called her "the girl." Joey had never met her. Mrs. McKnight told Joey on one of their trips to the doctor that Sean liked to be called "Mac," and that he, Joey, would think she was very pretty. Sarah McKnight loved her daughter, that was obvious, but it was also very clear that she hated her husband for driving "the girl" away. Somehow, even though it probably didn't bode well for Mac, Joey couldn't help wanting to meet her. He called his uncle, packed his go bag, and brought the car around front.

Between the scaffolding and the cables hung from the New World concert hall's ceiling, the Sky Walk project screamed out to John Ghostwalker as a Parkour playground. With each stage of construction there was something new to climb up, jump off, and/or swing from. Getting in after hours was easy, so was pausing the security tapes, so John had set about creating a number of unique and demanding trails. The cables and support girders had been chromed over, but as John found out the first time he grabbed onto one of them, even a tiny sliver of cracked chrome plating was a nasty shaped, razor sharp micro blade. He bought leather gloves that strapped tight around his wrist, and he was off and swinging like Spiderman.

The plexi-glass walkway section pieces were sorted and piled throughout the auditorium, and were scheduled to begin being installed in a week or two at most. The giant square washers and the nuts (also chrome plated) that would hold them in place at the end of each threaded cable were stacked in wooden crates on the stage, and John had inspected the washers carefully before he'd ever authorized the job foreman to sign for them. Sometimes, after a clandestine Parkour run around the hall, he would reopen one of the boxes and run his fingers carefully over several of the shiny steel plates before going home for the night. There wasn't going to be any Hyatt-like collapse on his watch.

Two days in the car with Edward McKnight was no picnic for Joey Beans. The man had become totally obsessed with a young man named Ghostwalker. "What kind of a name is that?" Joey wondered to himself as Edward's one-sided conversation in the backseat grew more paranoid and psychotic. Joey remembered seeing a beastly character named Golum talk to himself like this in the movie *Lord of the Rings*, and Golum's madness had led him to a very bad end. Joey couldn't imagine things going well for either Edward or the Ghostwalker guy he was fixated on.

Joey dutifully saw to their meals, arranged for each night's lodging, and called his uncle every chance he got.

"When are you doing to get me outta here, Uncle Louie? McKnight's all obsessed about some guy named Ghostwalker, like he's gonna whack him or something."

"You're almost done, Joey. Ghostwalker is the McKnight girl's boyfriend, but he doesn't matter. Our guys went through McKnight's home office and his big computer there after you left, and we've got all the stuff he needs to sign to withdraw our money and get it wired to our accounts. We'll fax it to you, and then you gotta get him to sign it."

"I can barely get him to eat or sleep, Uncle Louie, and you want me to ask him to sign over all the mob's money?"

"Well, no, Joey. The boss wants you to get him to sign over *all* the money....ours *and* his. But don't let on that last."

"Oh shit."

– The Ghostwalker File –

# Chapter 38: Hustle and Bustle

Mac, John, Abraham, and soon even Dan, were overwhelmed with interview requests. Orders were coming in from around the world, and Jacobs & Associates was swamped with inquiries about designing entire buildings around the Space Station concept. Resort complexes already under construction when the economy crashed had begun looking for ways to downsize on the opulence, and the Space Station offered them a way to reduce former room size footprints, thus adding select space for economy minded travelers in each hallway, and generally putting "more heads on beds" within the confines of buildings already set in concrete. Benny Lopez came up with the idea of using the same kind of foreclosed properties he'd been putting families in to create temporary dormitories for south Florida service workers, but mentioned it to a reporter before running it by anyone at Personal Space, Inc., so when that idea caught fire in the press, it just added to the commotional overload.

Custom built trailers soon carried Space Stations out of the factory like over sized kayaks at up to a half dozen at a time, and for the first few months, the 2-man installation crews were getting it all done. By the fourth month, they were flying in installer trainees from every major customer base, but still they could barely keep up. The workforce tripled in six months, the factory ran three shifts a day, and it appeared that foreign sales would likely catch up with domestic sales by the end of the first year. Oscar Wright had hired four new people just to handle dealership contract arrangements, two for domestic, and two for the foreign interests. They had the proverbial tiger by the tail, but the money was pouring in, and over 300 hundred homeless men and women in Miami would have a safe, clean, and comfortable new place to live by the end of the next calendar year.

There had been a few casualties along the way, however. No good thing is ever accomplished without them. They have become known in the American culture, thanks to yet another widely borrowed military euphemism, as "acceptable losses." One of the first was Parkour. Time, and then energy, simply disappeared. The next casualty was the Sunday afternoon Miccosukee picnic. At first, the weekly gathering was sacrificed in the name of rest, but rest was the next casualty, so another excuse was scheduled to be researched, but John and Mac were just too damn tired to think about it. Somewhere along the way, as sales and production rose, intimacy began to decline. In the beginning, their newly discovered sexual life was creatively woven into the increasingly complicated fabric of their lives with all the skill and determination that love has to offer. The complexity of the problem even led to some rather exotic, and even moderately risky, solutions that, for a short while anyway, added a dimension of excitement to their love making. But it wasn't long before the added wear and tear gave way to a kind of physical and emotional relief when a suitable time and a place were simply impossible to find.

"This isn't working for me."

When John saw the text message from Mac, his next breath caught in his throat. In his heart of hearts he knew that Life, the Universe, and Everything had spun out of control; he had even thought about it some. *When one ventures into the edge of the jungle and grabs a tiger by the tail, either they weren't thinking at all about the consequences, or, more likely, they thought that somehow the tiger would run in a more convenient direction. However, if the tiger chooses to run deeper into the jungle, the risks arising from letting go grow geometrically more terrifying. Along with the inherent danger of the tiger itself, one must consider the fact that they are hopelessly lost in the very place that every other tiger lives and hunts...not to mention the myriad other predators calling the place home. Logic, of course, dictates that one hold on for dear life. Seemingly, the only chance for survival rests in the frail hope that the tiger will eventually carry you back to the edge of the jungle.*

The phone calls started within the hour. When folks failed to reach Mac, they began calling John.

"What do you mean, you don't know where she is?" Abraham griped. "Do I have to do her job too?"

"Sorry to bother you, John," Fred Hoover said sheepishly, "but I need clarification about a travel voucher from Norway?"

"John? This is Dan. I'm still getting the hang of this cell phone. Do you know where Mac is?"

It went on all that day, and the next. While John attempted to put out as many of the fires as he could, he kept trying to reach Mac. Calls and text messages went unanswered. What little sleep he made time for, he took in Mac's memory foam bed. Each time he woke with a start, he reminded himself that he had gotten her back once before, he now knew where her Keys squat house was, and so he would get her back again...when the time was right.

At some point during the third day after Mac's disappearance, everyone received a telephone call from Bernie, Oscar Wright's secretary and office manager. Oscar was calling for a special board meeting by giving all the directors the required 48-hour notice. Bernie informed each of them as to the time they should call in to the office, and got an agreement of attendance from each of them in return. Nobody needed to ask. Somehow they all knew that the meeting would shed light on Mac's whereabouts. It was a long two days, and John made it worse by putting Abraham Jacobs and Dan Stone on notice that he would be unavailable during the second of those two days.

As promised, John turned off his phone and disappeared. For most of the Jacobs & Associates, Personal Space, Inc. and Space Station, LLC team members, it was the very first time they came to grips with the fact that they knew absolutely nothing about where John and Mac lived. Everyone naturally assumed they lived together somewhere in Brickell, but suddenly found it odd that there had never even been a mention of their actual address. That night, John called a cab and went home to his room over Nate's shop. He found Rachel sound asleep in his hammock, so he stretched out in his wheelchair recliner and sank almost immediately into the sleep of the dead. When he finally roused himself, he was alone and it was almost noon. After a wash-up and a shave, John walked next door and sat down for lunch with the Blackfeathers as if he'd never been away.

"How's that Space thing goin', John?" Nate asked between bites. "Sure been in the news a lot."

"A little too good," John said with a smile. "How's work?"

"A little too slow," Nate said, "but no layoffs yet. I almost took a job at your factory, but they only wanted people for night shift. Too old for that."

"I hear you there," John said. "Lately I feel like I'm a hundred. Speaking of that, Rachel could I kick you back in the house for one night? "

"Of course, John. You OK? Where's Mac?"

"Well, that's the thing. I don't think this corporate life agrees with either of us, but, as usual, she figured it out first. Then she split."

"You're going to go after her, aren't you?" Rachel asked.

– The Ghostwalker File –

"Like night follows day."

## Chapter 39: The Corporate Shuffle

When John woke up the following day, and joined the Blackfeathers for breakfast, he once again felt more buoyant, and less like he was drowning in his life. He was no longer particularly interested in the board meeting scheduled for later in the morning. He would attend, but it was going to be what it was going to be. There was something so primal about each and every household in which he had grown up sharing meals, and the Blackfeather's were, in many ways, an amalgam of what was best about the Miccosukee tribe. John was an amalgam of what he had learned from all of them. Every tribe of human beings, everywhere around the globe, began with an understanding of personal and corporate prioritization. They had to. When survival was at stake every day, ignoring the lessons about basic priorities meant physical death, of the individual, and of the tribe. Community was everything. In America, at least, the "rugged individual" came to be valued more and more, and the stakes involved with basic survival sometimes seemed less.

New rules of prioritization spring from relative safety and growing affluence, and little by little, the old rules can fade away. Community seemed less important in mainstream America. At Haskell Indian Nations University, John had distanced himself, as he always distanced himself from most things, from active participation in the effort to overcome the fading away of tradition. But community was strong there, and he had always appreciated its power from safe distance. Haskell, at its heart and soul, was about learning by remembering. Native Americans could not afford to take for granted the sovereignty of the tribe. John had slept and studied in a sanctuary that was itself an ancient classroom that was not only about the past, it *was* the past, and though he succeeded in keeping his primary focus on moving forward as fast as possible, there was no way for him to leave all the lessons behind. He carried them with him every day...even when he seemed to forget them completely.

One by one, the directors of Personal Space, Inc. called in and were asked to hold on. Grandmother Renee muted her TV, but was still watching the Oprah channel while she waited. Dan Stone lay on his back on the hand woven oval carpet in front of her easy chair, holding his new cell phone to his ear, humming along with the hold music. The rocking chair creaked softly as John sat quietly with his eyes closed. His Bluetooth earpiece glowed with a tiny red L.E.D. light, and his cell phone rested on Grandmother Renee's TV tray table, right next to the two new Milky Way bars. Life, the Universe and Everything was about to change, but under this roof, that was OK.

"Only a crazy man fights change in a world that will never stop changing." It was another of Grandmother Renee's most oft-repeated mantras. "A sane man learns, remembers, and moves on."

The two men in her living room were living proof that crazy men could become sane, and John didn't begrudge Dan Stone a bit for learning it first.

"Ladies, Gentlemen," Oscar's voice interrupted their reverie and/or their Oprah, "can I have a motion to forego the reading of the minutes from our last meeting?"

"So moved," Abraham Jacobs responded immediately.

"May I have a second to the motion?"

"I second the motion," said Ted Connors, the "Sultan of Snooze." Ted was the fourth partner in Space Station, LLC, so any possible change in the state of his new found cash flow was of far more concern to him than the minutes of the last Personal Space, Inc. board meeting he'd slept through.

"I have a motion and a second that the reading of the minutes of the last board meeting be omitted," Oscar said. "All in favor say 'aye.'"

Everyone said 'aye' in unison. John thought he heard Mac's 'aye' in the chorus and smiled to himself.

"Opposed? The motion is passed. Is there any old business to discuss?"

You could have heard a pin drop for the next ten seconds. It's quite likely no one breathed. Oscar moved on. "Under new business, I'd like to begin with a few organizational items. First, Sean McKnight has resigned as the President of Personal Space, Inc., effective immediately, and has drafted the following motion: 'I move that Grandmother Renee Persons be named Honorary President of Personal Space, Inc., and that Dan Stone be named Acting President, effective immediately.' The motion has been read," Oscar said. "Do I have a second?"

It seemed in the silence that no one had yet drawn a breath, but John jumped in. "I second that motion."

"The motion has been made and seconded. Is there any discussion?"

John held his breath, and made his best ever attempt at prayer.

"All in favor say 'aye,'" Oscar said, perhaps more

quickly than he normally did, and the somewhat hesitant 'ayes' filled the phone line. "All opposed?"

John prayed again.

"The motion passed," Oscar said. His relief was obviously as great as John's. "May I extend my congratulations to both Ms. Persons and Mr. Stone, and with their permission, I'd like to move to the next item of new business."

"You go right ahead, child," Grandmother Renee said.

"Sure," Dan said, "that's OK with me too."

As silly as it sounded, even as it occurred to him, John was certain that he had heard Mac's sigh of relief. He knew she was smiling too. As Oscar dealt with the necessary details, motions, discussions, and votes came and went, and the meeting adjourned as every prior meeting had adjourned. The world had not ended, and no one had been eaten by the tiger. Several minutes later, John quietly slid the rocker back a bit and snapped a cell phone picture of Grandmother Renee in her chair and Dan Stone on his back...both of them fast asleep. He texted the shot to Mac with a two word message: "very cool." Analogies are only as good as one's point of view, John decided as he continued rocking, and he tried to imagine Mac's.

*When one ventures into the edge of the jungle and grabs a tiger by the tail, either they weren't thinking at all about the consequences, or, more likely, they thought that somehow the tiger would run in a more convenient direction. However, if the tiger chooses to run deeper into the jungle, the risks arising from letting go grow geometrically more terrifying. Along with the inherent danger of the tiger itself, one must consider the fact that they could become hopelessly lost in the very place that every other tiger lives and hunts...not to mention the myriad other predators calling the place home. Logic, of course, dictates that one let go as unobtrusively and as quickly as possible, and begin walking back in the direction from whence they came. Only by following the trail they had just blazed, was there any hope of returning safely to the edge of the jungle.*

– Kevin Robinson –

# Chapter 40: Special Delivery

Edward McKnight looked more insane than usually, dressed as he was in a thousand dollar suit, Gucci shoes, and a yellow hard hat. Joey sat in the car and watched from across the street as Edward strolled nonchalantly back and forth past the receiving dock at the New Word Center. It was lunch hour. McKnight first glanced at his watch, then down the Miami Beach side street, over and over while he paced. "So that's why I always got busted," Joey laughed to himself. "I didn't dress up fancy enough!"

When the big white Mercedes delivery truck driver stopped and put on his flashers, Edward McKnight hopped up onto the cab's running board, leaned in close for a whispered conversation, and pressed a huge wad of cash into the man's hand. The driver gave him a hearty thumbs-up and began backing up to the loading dock. Joey had been ordered to stay in the car, but just like his orders about getting McKnight to sign a dozen fax documents, he just wasn't having any luck in the following orders department.

From behind a tree at the edge of the sculpture garden, Joey watched as the truck off-loaded a pallet of four wooden crates with an electric hand truck. Edward had moved off the loading dock and into the building, but returned and waved the driver to follow him. As soon as they were out of sight, Joey scampered up onto the loading dock and followed them through a door, down a hallway, and through a second door marked "Back Stage." From a cracked opening in that door, Joey watched as the freight driver lowered his pallet to the stage floor, and picked up a similar pallet nearby. As Joey ran back down the hallway to avoid being seen when McKnight and the driver started back towards him, he heard parts of an argument between the two men.

"Hell no!" the driver said. "I can't take this stuff anywhere."

"I'll pay you more!" Edward insisted.

"It's grand theft if I leave here with these crates. Not going to happen."

Joey ducked into a restroom on the loading dock and watched as the driver clearly recognized that he was dealing with a crazy man, dropped the second pallet off in the corner, and made a hasty retreat. McKnight, beet red with agitation, looked around frantically before spotting a canvas tarp folded up next to the out-to-lunch receiving clerk's desk. He shook open the tarp and carefully covered the pallet of wooden crates he had obviously hoped would be gone by now. When he was finished, and had piled a few odd items on top of his creation, he hopped off the loading dock and crossed the street.

"Shit!" Joey said to himself as Edward looked both ways down the street for him. "Now what?"

He knew he couldn't leave the way he came in without being seen, and he needed a couple seconds, at least, to cross the back of the loading dock to the hallway door. That was his only hope, so he tried to time Edward's turns this way and that as best he could before bursting out of hiding and charging through the hallway door. He retraced his steps to the backstage door, ducked into the concert hall, ran up the aisle, and entered the lobby trying to act like he belonged there. Freedom was several sets of double glass doors to his right, and he prayed he would trip no alarms as he strolled out one of them and walked east through the sculpture garden, blending into the Miami Beach lunchtime crowd. By the time he walked west back down the side street where the car was parked, and waved to Edward like nothing was the matter, he was relieved not to see any signs of security or the police.

"Hi Boss! I had to pee. Everything go OK in there?"

"Well, yes, I guess it did. I want a room at the old Cadillac Hotel," he said. "It should be a few blocks that way."

"Yes, sir, Boss," Joey said as he held the door. "I'll get right on it."

The "old Cadillac Hotel" was now a Marriott, but had been renovated in true Miami Beach - Deco Drive tradition, but the old silver Cadillac sign still hung over the lobby entrance doors. Joey booked two rooms, got his boss unpacked, and convinced Edward to buy them lunch at the Carraba's next door. Joey had mentioned the faxed documents the night before, insisting that the Baltimore mob boss had been very clear about having Edward sign them immediately, but if his hard sell approach had any effect at all, Joey couldn't see it. McKnight had just stared blankly at the Weather Channel without any emotion on his face throughout Joey's impassioned spiel, and then when Joey wound down, said: "Goodnight, Joey. See you in the morning."

Joey's next approach was going to be Edward's favorite wine, a California red that cost nearly two hundred dollars a bottle. When he called down for a late lunch reservation at Carraba's, Joey instructed them to keep the stuff coming by the bottle as it was his boss's birthday, but that any mention of the subject would ruin the occasion.

It appeared to go very well until they were on their third bottle and Edward began singing "London Bridge is Falling Down" as he picked at his tiramisu. Joey figured it was time to get Edward back to his room and get him to sign the fax pages, so he scribbled the boss's room number on the bill, left a sizable tip, grabbed up the half empty bottle of wine, and ushered the swaying Irishman out of the restaurant and into an elevator.

Though Joey grew up hearing stories involving drunken Irishmen, he'd never dealt with one before. On the other hand, he'd lost count of the drunken Italian-American friends he'd helped home, so how different could it be? About halfway to their floor, Edward stopped singing.

"Tha was, ah, good wine, eh, Joey?"

"Yes, sir, it was," Joey said, watching for signs that his boss might throw up on him.

"You've got some more there. I can see it. You wouldn't hold back on me would you?"

"Never, boss," Joey said. "As soon as we get you up to your room, and we get those damn papers signed, it's all yours."

"Good!" Edward said with a creepy smile. He was singing "Ring Around the Rosie" as they made their way down the hallway and into his room, and as Joey eased him into the desk chair, McKnight seemed particularly pleased with his rendition of the "and they all fall down" refrain. But try as he might, Joey couldn't get his otherwise fixated boss to sign anything.

## Chapter 41: Behind the Scenes

The next morning Joey made himself coffee and read the newspaper which had been slid under his door. He was surprised to see an article about the New World Center and the Sky Walk that was in its final phase of the construction. Opening night was just over a week away. The reality of what his boss had done, and what would happen as a result, hit him full in the face. Like it or not, he was involved. Being stuck in Miami Beach with a crazy man, being unable to comply with his uncle's instructions, and now, being involved with what seemed to him like a terrorist attack made Joey feel very vulnerable. His scrapes with the law through the years were very minor by comparison, and his Uncle Louie was always able to make them go away, but this was something else altogether. He pulled out his wallet and slid out one of the last items he copped from the McKnight house after Sarah's death. As he stared at the picture of Sean McKnight that he'd found on Sarah's nightstand, he had to admit that her mother was right. He did think Mac was pretty, and he didn't want to be even partially responsible for her death, or for the deaths of anyone else at the upcoming concert. But, be that as it may, he had no idea what to do about it.

When it became clear that his boss wasn't going anywhere—at least not until after he'd seen his master plan through to its end—Joey spent his days trying to figure out what to do. He discovered the boardwalk which stretched for miles along the beach behind the hotel, and spent hours strolling along with the beach bunnies, the joggers, the tourists and the local Hassidic Jews. It was very unlike Baltimore, and he liked it, but he was becoming more frustrated too. His first dilemma was whether or not to call his uncle and really fill him in. Uncle Louie had, thus far, made it very clear that he didn't care what McKnight was up to, but who else could Joey call?

He was unaware that he was aimlessly walking in circles, muttering to himself right in from of a long wooden bench full of mildly amused elderly locals, until a tall man in a dark suit took his elbow, flashed open a black leather badge case, and said: "Walk with me, Joey Beans. We need to talk."

"Mac has never had a community before," Grandmother Renee said. "Some, certainly too many, human beings have forgotten this story about who we are. Without community, we are adrift. We have no real stories upon which to build our lives, we have no ceremonies to unite us and to feed us spiritually, we have no true healing, and we have no sense of communal rhythm to maintain our balance as we move forward in this life. Only our shared stories lead the way to these things."

"I feel all these things in my life, Grandmother, " John said as he rocked next to her easy chair, "and we have all shared these things with Mac, but she is not at peace here. "

"Her wind blows her elsewhere at present, this is true,"

Grandmother Renee said, "but Mac is one of us now. Not because of anything she did, but simply because we made it so. Just as you are one of us, so is she."

"I hope she knows that," John said.

"She knows, child. She knows."

Special Agent Taylor Maine led Joey several blocks south before turning west down a side street and opening the doors of a heavily tinted window van.

"Seems to us like you've gotten yourself tangled up in something very unpleasant, Joey," the FBI man said after introducing Joey to the other agent in the truck. "And Agent Franks here is convinced that you're an equal partner in the whole deal. If he's right, we should turn you over to Homeland Security and let them sort it out with you down in Guantanamo."

Agent Franks shrugged his shoulders and his expression said: "What other answer could there be?" Joey turned a lighter shade of pale.

"But I'm not convinced yet," Agent Maine went on. "I've been watching you, Joey Beans. Seems to me that you're looking for a way out, and that maybe your Uncle Louie hasn't been very open to that. Am I right on this one, or should I defer to Agent Franks and move on to the next case?"

## Chapter 42: Loose Ends

Several days later, overnight shipments arrived for all but three members of the Personal Space, Inc.'s board of directors. Inside was an assignment of ownership rights in Space Station, LLC. Mac, it turned out, had divested of her 25% ownership by dividing it equally amongst those receiving the packages. The other three principle owners, John Ghostwalker, Abraham Jacobs, and Ted Conners had been excluded, but everyone else now owned a small piece of the profit pie. Based on projected earnings, that in itself was no small matter, but if one took into account the growing list of international companies making not-so-subtle inquiries as to buy-out opportunities, even those small ownership slices represented a lot of potential pie.

It was all going to be OK. He was on the path, so it was all good. John began checking off items on his mental list throughout the remainder of the day. Everyone at Jacobs & Associates was relieved to see him back at his desk. The Maestro's Sky Mall was debuting the next night, complete with a performance by Miami's own Seraphic Fire, and no one wanted to think about John being AWOL for that. He had assured everyone, several times each, that he would be present, especially after receiving a phone call from Frank Ghary.

"Are you trying to give Abraham a heart attack?" Frank asked him. "He called me all in a tizzy."

"He loves tizzies," John replied. "He thrives on them."

"Well then I'll see you tomorrow night?"

"Yes, you will. I'm actually looking forward to it."

The steadily relaxing glances just outside his glass walled office wouldn't have been so relaxed if they could have seen his computer screen as John updated his resume, printed it out, and stuffed it into an envelope along with a heartfelt cover letter. On his way over to Perricone's Marketplace & Café to pick up his lunch, John dropped the envelope in a mailbox, shaking his head and laughing at himself as he did so. He settled into his old park bench, and between bites of his roast beef sandwich, he pulled out his old architect's box and began sketching the building going up across the street to the south. When he finished eating, he made two light sketches on the recycled cardboard sandwich box and then traded his mechanical pencil for an X-ACTO knife and started carving out his two drawings. In order to complete the task, John waved down a cab, went down to the marina store by Brickell Key, and bought two tiny rubber alligators before returning to his office and all the relieved looks that entailed.

"We good for tomorrow night?" Abraham asked him for the tenth time.

"We're good, boss. Relax. But do you still have any of those bistro seat tickets?"

"Damn! I forgot I even had those. Yes, I've got four of them. Why?"

"I'd like to buy two of them from you."

"Forget that! They're all yours. There wouldn't be a tomorrow night if it wasn't for you."

"Thank you."

John returned to his office and called Rachel. "Has Billy asked you out yet?"

"Almost, I think. But not yet. Why?"

"I didn't say anything in front of your folks, but I thought I sensed a turn in the tide the other day, like you wouldn't mind if he did?"

"Yeah, so?"

"So ask him out. There will be two very cool tickets waiting for you at the Will Call window at the New World Center tomorrow night. Tell him you want to support my project there, and that you don't want to drive into Miami Beach on your own. Anything to make him think he's stepping up without worrying about getting shot down."

"Why are you doing this?"

"Because guys are idiots sometimes when it comes to smart, attractive women, and I don't want you to ever be afraid of acting like a smart, attractive woman. Tell him to dress up. Oh, and if you have a long dress, you probably want to wear it."

"OK," Rachel said. "I can do that."

"Good. See you tomorrow night." John checked another item off his list, and dialed Dan Stone.

"Hello, John? I love that this phone says who's calling!"

"Hi Dan," John said laughing. "Are you busy tonight? I'd like to take you to dinner. Can you get a cab into Brickell and meet me at my work?"

"Sure thing! I'll call Grandmother Renee and tell her I won't be over tonight. She'll be thrilled that I'm hangin' out with you. She's proud as hell of you."

"I know," John said. "She's a sweetie, and she's proud as hell of you too."

"Yeah, how about that? See you in an hour or so."

"Great!" Check.

John's next call was to Baltimore. "Hi, Bernie. Can I set up an appointment for a short chat with Oscar sometime?"

"You bet," Bernie said, "but he's just back from the courthouse, and as far as I know, he's free right now. If now's good for you, I'll ask him?"

"Sure. Thanks."

"John, how are you?" Oscar said when he came on the line. "What can I do for you?"

"As Grandmother Renee might say, 'Same. Same.' What you did for Mac with Space Station, LLC, except with a couple of personal tweaks."

"Mac talk to you about this?"

"Not a word," John said. "Haven't heard a peep out of her since that deep sigh of relief, and a few 'ayes' during the last board meeting. Was she up there with you, Oscar?"

"I'm not supposed to say."

"That's good enough for me. Do I need to come up for anything?"

"Nope. It's all on the computer. Just tell me about the changes, and I'll overnight it down for your signature. You sure about this?"

"Never surer about anything in my life."

"Damned if Mac didn't say you'd do this. She's amazing, that one."

"Yes she is, Oscar. Thanks for everything." Check.

John saw Dan walk through the front door, so he shut off the office light and headed up the hall to meet him. By the time he got there, Dan and Mandy were chatting it up like old buddies. John had never seen her smile before. No sign of the hand over the mouth, no nervous snorting. The middle aged woman was aglow, looking positively radiant, and Dan was so charming that John thought he'd walked into a movie scene. He paused for a moment and just soaked it in. When Dan looked up and saw him, John walked up and put his arm around the old vet's shoulder.

"Mandy giving you a hard time, Dan? She can be a pit bull."

"No, no, John. Quite the opposite, I assure you. You know how I can get to talkin'. This young lady has been waiting patiently for me to shut up."

"Why I was doing no such thing!" Mandy said as the blush crept over her face.

"Mandy Hawkins, meet my dear friend and mentor, Dan Stone," John said. "Dan, Mandy is the brain center of this modest enterprise. We'd all be lost without her."

"Pleased to meet you, Mandy."

"Same here," she said as the growing blush took five years off her appearance.

"Now, before Dan and I set out on a previous engagement, perhaps the two of you could do me a favor? The boss pushed two last minute tickets off on me for the New World Center deal tomorrow night, and I'm supposed to fill two bistro seats somehow. Any chance you two would take them off my hands?"

"Bistro seats? Oh my!" Mandy said, "Those are $250 each."

"I believe it would be rude not to help John out on this," Dan said to Mandy. "What about it?"

It wasn't even close to being on John's list, but he checked it off anyway.

## Chapter 43: *Mi Casa es Su Casa*

"This is good chow," Dan said, "I haven't eaten out a lot in the last few years, and Lord knows I haven't had a date since the eighties. What have you gotten me into, Master John?"

"Good things, I hope," John said, "but if it turns out not to be good, just walk away. No harm, no foul."

"I hear you. I take one day at a time."

They sat under a blue and red umbrella on the concrete mall outside the ground floor café under the Brickell Town Towers, and when they were finished eating, John took Dan for a leisurely walk past the rest of the shops and out into the back alley.

"Always look both ways here, Dan, then you take these stairs. Once you're in the stairway, at least in the daytime, stay over in the shadow against the wall, away from the window openings."

Dan followed silently for several stories, but then said, "Good Lord, John, I know I'm a bit out of shape, but are we training for the Olympics here?"

"Sorry," John laughed, and slowed his pace. "This is where Mac and I live, and nobody on earth knows about it but us, and now you. But I know you'll get it, and I'd trust you with my life. I just need a favor."

"Name it," Dan said between heavy breaths, "and if I survive this climb, I'll do whatever you need."

"Thanks, Dan. I was hoping you'd say that."

When they reached the fifteenth floor, John took a key chain out of his pocket, unlocked the fire escape door, and opened it a crack. "You can see all the way down the hall without going inside," he said quietly. "Always make sure it's clear."

"Got it."

John led the way inside, and pointed to the security camera mounted over their heads. "As long as you don't go past that first apartment door there on the right, the security guys can't see you. I'm in here."

"Damn!" Dan said when John pushed in on the wall and the invisible door popped open. "They didn't call you Ghostwalker for nothing. This is just frickin' cool!"

They walked down the short, widening entryway and into John's apartment, and Dan just stood turning circles in the center of the small room as John opened the louvers on the balcony doors. "Don't go out there during the daytime," he said, "but these open like a closet door, and the balcony is pretty awesome at night."

"How'd you get all this stuff up here? And where do you sleep?"

"A lot of Olympic training," John laughed. He walked over to the book shelves, slid the two protruding center sections to either side, and pulled down the Murphy bed. "What do you think?"

"Never seen anything like it!" Dan said. "You are amazing."

"No," John said, "I'm just a recluse at heart." He placed the key chain with the rubber alligator dangling on it in Dan's hand. "It's yours if you want it." Hanging beside the gold fire door key was a cardboard key with the number

"15" on it. Dan looked at it and laughed. "Just a symbolic gesture," John said, "but I thought you might like to have a place in town once in a while."

"Thanks," Dan said, his voice tight in his throat. "Guess this means you're headed out?"

"In a few days. Let's go upstairs."

After showing Dan Mac's place, John placed the second rubber alligator key chain in his friend's hand. The cardboard key said "16." "This is for Rachel, if she wants it. She's commuting to the University of Miami, and I'm going to tell her to see you if she'd like to stay in the city sometimes. But you've got to school her about not drawing attention. Her new boyfriend's a cop, so make sure she gets it, OK?"

"You got it."

"Thanks." Check.

The following day when John showed up at work, Mandy was so bubbly and talkative everyone in the office was more than a little unnerved. He just smiled, and enjoyed the spotlight being elsewhere. Abraham was flitting, here, there, and everywhere, and if he popped into John's office to say nothing at all once, he did it eight times before lunch. And that was fine. John's fitting was scheduled for 11:30 a.m., and when the man from Brickell Tux showed up, everyone found some excuse to walk by his glass-walled office at least once. Seeing John Ghostwalker in his first ever tuxedo was a spectacle not to be missed, and no one failed to notice the dramatic effect. The scruffy, polyester wearing country boy looked like the next James Bond, and one female associate told a co-worker that she'd have to "do him" right there in his office if he left the tux on much longer.

John asked the tailor to snap a couple photos with his cell phone, thanked him, and changed back into his street clothes before heading out for lunch at Allan Morris Brickell Park. Back on his bench, he sent one of the photos to Mac with the message "sow's ear in silk purse." She didn't answer, but somehow he knew she was smiling.

## Chapter 44: Grand Openings

A limo picked John and Abraham up at 4:30 p.m., and then it swung by the Marriott Biscayne Bay to pick up Frank Ghary. It was a short drive across the Intracoastal Waterway to the New World Center, and both the symphony hall lobby and the adjacent park were filled to capacity. The big screen in the sculpture park showed what was going on inside, and as the three men left the limo and headed down the sidewalk, they could see a gaggle of press and a number of Miami-Dade movers and shakers already gathered around the symbolic red ribbon that adorned the south elevator.

In the shadows at the edge of the sculpture park, Edward McKnight alternated between staring at the Skywalk as it appeared on the giant video screen and scanning the entrance sidewalk for new arrivals. When he saw John Ghostwalker coming down the sidewalk, he felt the thrill of genuine excitement, and whether it was a conscious act or not, he probably wasn't counting pocket change with his right hand. His hand stopped moving, however, when the limo pulled away without having delivered his only child. Agitation replaced foreplay, and he began rocking back and forth where he stood. "OK," he whispered to himself. "It's OK. One thing at a time."

"After you," Abraham said, holding the door for his companions.

"The show must go on," Frank said, patting John reassuringly on the shoulder. "It'll be over before you know it."

"God, I hope so," John said as he passed through the door and into a barrage of camera flashes. Fortunately, most of the cameras and questions were aimed at Frank Ghary, and John marveled at how the old architect handled the press as easily as he might handle a few overly enthusiastic grandchildren. The ribbon got cut, the reception seemed to drag on forever, but eventually the press cleared out and the audience filed in.

There were long lines at each of the elevators as nearly everyone wanted to traverse the Skywalk before the show, but about three dozen of them got to stay up there. The "Bistro seats" on the south side were actually seats at the permanent bistro, where a select few could order food and watch the concert from above while they sat at their tall plexi-glass bar tables. The "Park seats," on the far side of the Skywalk were actual park benches made of plexi-glass, strewn amongst various potted flora. Should these folks choose to nosh, a quaint organic hot dog stand was nestled in the landscaping by the north elevator to accommodate them. John was seated in the front row on the main floor, but he saw Rachel and Billy greeting Dan and Mandy up in the bistro above him to his right. They had obviously agreed to share a table, and sat chatting enthusiastically. Rachel noticed him watching, pointed him out to the others, and they all waved, just as John snapped their picture with his cell phone. Frank and Abraham noticed the flash, looked up, and joined John as he waved back.

"Who are they?" Frank asked.

"Friends and family," John said. "God bless friends and family."

"Amen," Frank and Abraham said in unison.

Back outside, Edward McKnight was literally vibrating with anger and frustration. "It should have worked," he whispered with spittle flying out of his mouth. He intensified his self-stim rocking until his forehead hit the stainless steel sculpture with each forward motion. "Why isn't it falling down?"

"Because it's not your day, Ed," Agent Maine said as he slapped on a pair of handcuffs, "it's just not your day at all."

The house lights dimmed, and the audience grew still. A lone shadow moved to center stage, and a clear soprano voice echoed through the symphony hall as a spotlight grew out of nothing around her. One by one, spotlights and angelic a cappella voices joined in from every corner of the great room and its various balconies. Three of the spotlights shot upwards in succession as singers appeared in the Bistro, the Park, and then in the plexi-glass walkway directly above the stage where a tall, lanky baritone, seemingly suspended in mid-air, brought the sound of thunder to the perfect harmonies. No one noticed that a chamber orchestra had somehow manifested itself on stage until the violins and the cello crept into the mix like storm clouds from afar. Intermittent lights in the Skywalk became lightning, and many audience members instinctively held out one hand, palm up, when their minds could not distinguish between the apparent sounds of rain and the majestic power of the trained human voice along with a rhythmic clapping of hands on thighs. As was their custom, Seraphic Fire mesmerized its audience, refusing to release their magical hold for over an hour and a half. Even outside in the sculpture park, on blankets, next to strollers, in lawn chairs, and sometimes standing shoulder to shoulder staring at the big screen, people were transfixed. Time became meaningless, and music became the air they all breathed together.

## Chapter 45: More Loose Ends

The thumbs up text from Agent Maine read like a prayer. Edward McKnight would never hurt anyone, ever. But it had been much too close. The far-below-minimum grade nuts had been spray painted silver instead of being chrome plated like the aircraft grade originals, and John liked to think that he, or someone, would have spotted that. But with the frantic intensity and the hectic pace of those last few days of construction, John could not be sure of that. He thanked the spirits of his people, and the spirits of all human beings, for the blessing of life.

Perhaps John had built his great building after all. He could not imagine anything bigger or taller that could match the feeling of satisfaction that filled his soul. Much to the chagrin of those around him, John had snapped several pictures for Mac throughout the performance. He just didn't care what anyone thought. As the stunned crowd reluctantly filed out after two encores, John joined his friends at the Bistro.

"What did you think?" he asked them.

"Who would believe it if we told them?" Dan laughed.

"Absolutely breathtaking," Mandy said. It appeared as if she was totally unaware of either how long or how tightly she had been clutching Dan's hand. The man's fingers were as white as a corpse.

"You dreamed this thing up?" Billy said, shaking his head. "I don't know what to say, except thanks for letting us share this night with you."

"You did good, bro." Rachel said as she hugged him. "And you look pretty spiffy too. And oh my God, thanks for the tip about the dress!"

The next day his phone rang all day long as Personal Space, Inc. board members called to thank him. Because 80% of John's ownership had been divided amongst them, their ownership percentage in Space Station, LLC had nearly doubled, and while some just gushed with gratitude, others like Grandmother Renee and Dan Stone seemed to assume that there had been some mistake and offered to assign it all right back to him on the spot. John respectfully declined, and urged them to stay the course, and make sure that the business never stopped helping the not-for-profit provide shelter for those in need. As for the last 20%, the other three callers that day were more baffled, perhaps, but no less grateful. The Rosario twins called first.

"That factory that's been on TV?" Jose said. "Where those cool little tricked out housing units are made, we each own a piece of that?"

"Yes, you do."

"Why for?" Emanuel asked.

"Because you gave me two of the best things in life: Parkour and friendship. I will always treasure both."

"Hell, bro," Jose said, "you dyin' or something?"

"No," John laughed, "I'm not dying. I am going away for awhile, but I'll see you guys whenever I'm back in town, OK?"

"You got it!" Jose said.

"Thanks, brotherman," Emanuel said. "That's a real nice thing you did for us."

"Wait 'till you've got to stay awake during the board meetings…then you might think differently!"

"Hell no, man," Jose said, "we were born to do business!"

Check.

When Marion Blackfeather called, she said nothing about the letters she and Nate had each received. She just asked John over for dinner, and he gladly accepted her invitation. After all, he had just given away the keys to his apartment. He had to go somewhere.

"I had to ask Rachel what a 'voluntary proviso' was," Nate said over supper. "Sure helps to have a smart-ass college kid around the house!" Rachel kicked him under the table and everybody laughed. "So what's the catch?"

"Daddy!" Rachel said. "You could at least say 'thank you' first."

"You wouldn't think so if the proviso was that I keep you locked up in the broom closet 'till you're 21, would you now?"

"Daddy, you're impossible!"

"Enough you two," Marion said. "What do you want us to do, John?"

Lots of folks are hurting. Banks aren't lending. So I was hoping that you guys might consider setting ten percent of whatever your ownership in Space Station, LLC brings in aside for a community loan fund, where folks wouldn't have to pay interest when they got in a bind and needed a loan."

"That's a wonderful idea!" Marion said, as Nate and Rachel nodded enthusiastically.

"Oscar Wright will help you set up a small not-for-profit corporation so the money you, or anybody else, donates to the fund will be tax deductible, and you can write it off against your income taxes. I'll pitch in, and I'll ask everybody involved with both projects to chip in when they can."

"What should we call it?" Nate asked.

"Anything you want. Just call Oscar when you're ready."

"Well, see, Rachel?" Nate laughed. "Now that we know you're safe and free, we can thank John in good conscience!"

"Dad! You are so bad."

Check.

The next-to-the-last item on John's mental list could be a little rough. He walked into work on Monday morning and parked himself in front of Abraham's desk.

"You look serious," Abraham said.

"Well," John said, "I have a favor to ask, but before I ask it, I wanted to tell you how much I appreciate all you've done for me. You feel more like a friend to me than a boss, so if you say 'no,' I want you to know that I'll be fine with it."

"This must be bad," Abraham said. "What do you want?"

"Two things, actually. I'd like a leave of absence without pay. Maybe two weeks? And then I'd like to work part time and remotely. Almost everything we do is on computer. I can do it from anywhere."

"Well," Abraham said, "there's actually an office pool going on for what day you take off after Mac. I had last Monday, so I had to buy another slot. Thanks for not bolting then, really. I figured I'd lose you, because even I wouldn't trade Mac for me! You put this firm on a much bigger map, John Ghostwalker, and I'm proud to have you aboard for as long as you want to stay."

"Thanks, boss." Check.

John took a cab back out to the Blackfeathers, had dinner there, and then crossed the backyard to visit Grandmother Renee.

"There you are, my child! Come in and sit down. Daniel and I were about to watch NCIS, but I'll set it to record."

"Hey Dan!" John said, gentling poking the old vet with his toe as he stepped over him to hug the tiny woman. "How are you, Grandmother?"

"I am wonderful. I don't exactly know what you and Mac have done for me, but Dan says it might be quite a lot of money, so he and I are going to help Nathan and Marion with their new project. They're very excited!"

"That's good, I'm glad that you guys will be helping them. About the money, at the end of every quarter—March, June, September, and December—the accountant tallies up the company's profit/loss sheet. If there's a profit, 50% of it goes into the company's operating fund, and the other 50% gets divided up among the owners. You're one of the owners so if things keep on the way they're going, you'll get four checks every year. Also, if a bigger company comes up with an offer that the majority of owners agree to, and you all sell the company, than you'll probably get one big check, or maybe a smaller check, then monthly or quarterly checks from the new owners. Oscar will always advise you anytime you have questions."

"Well, child, that's a lot to think about, but since I have everything I need, it will be fun to do some good with anything else that comes in."

"You do more good in a day, Grandmother, than most folks do in a lifetime," John laughed, "but I'll have fun watching you."

"I'm glad you will, and I'm also glad you stopped by tonight because I have something for you; well, actually, for both of you together."

Dan sat up and John settled into the rocker, both wondering what Grandmother Renee was up to.

Grandmother Renee lifted the edge of her *O Magazine* and pulled two brown envelopes out from underneath it. She handed one to each of them. "Anything can happen, I always say, and sometimes it actually does."

Dan and John looked at the envelopes, then at each other.

"Who is 'Person A,' Grandmother?" Dan asked as he dug his fingernail up under the seal and tore open his envelope.

"Why you are, child."

"So I'm 'Person B?'" John asked.

"Yes you are."

Each of the men pulled a tri-folded piece of paper out of their envelope, and once unfolded, each very technical looking document had a small zip-lock bag stapled in one upper corner.

"Well, Doctor John," Dan said, "you're the college man. This is all Greek to me. What does it mean?"

"I have no idea," John confessed, "but the hair in the bag looks like mine."

"Mine too," Dan said.

"DNA, Grandmother?" John said looking up. "Is this a DNA test?"

"Why, child, you get a gold star!" The white-haired woman said, beaming. "They are, indeed, DNA tests, and they confirm what I've been thinking for quite some time: that our little ghost child did, in fact, come to us for a reason. His father was one of us, and his mother—whomever she may be and whatever she might have been running from—must have hoped that her baby would find his father one day. And today is that day!"

Both men seemed to stop breathing, and they looked at each other, as if for the first time. Tears came simultaneously for all three of them as Grandmother Renee laid out her theory and the timeline that supported it. Dan's ill-fated dream date in 1987, and John's birth in 1988, some unknown day just prior to being found at the entrance to the Museum Village, it all just fit.

John moved to the floor and kept whispering "Wow!" and as they embraced each other, Dan kept saying "I have a son!"

Grandmother Renee was more than a little pleased with

herself, but eventually she stopped talking and just stared at them, soaking it all in.

"You even have her hair," Dan said between sobs, "and that little dent thing on your nose. And still, it just never occurred to me."

"Who would have ever thought?" John laughed. "Oh, except Grandmother Renee!"

"Indeed!" she said. "My work here is almost finished, but first there is one other important matter. When are you going after Mac? I do love that child."

"So do I," John said, "and I'm leaving tomorrow. I just came by to get your blessing and kiss your head for good luck."

"Oh you sassy child!" she said as she wrapped her frail arms around both of them. "Neither one of you has ever taken a step in your lives without my blessing on you, and don't you forget it!"

"Thank you, Grandmother. I will never forget." Check, and double check.

## Chapter 46: The Heart and Soul of the Hunter

 

John and his dad had talked late into the night, long after Grandmother Renee had bid them goodnight and gone to her bed. He told Dan about all his plans, and the old vet's pride and approval were obvious. At sunrise, they hugged for the hundredth time and John set off. Loose ends were tied up, John was free of all obligations, and he arrived at the bus stop moments before the first bus of the day came by. It was a short hop to Homestead, and then, for $2.50 he could take another bus all the way to Key West, or anywhere in between. The trip would take him, first, through "the eighteen mile stretch" of Everglades, into Key Largo, and then from one island to another, across water that was more shades of blue than he had ever imagined possible. Mile Marker 61 was halfway to Key West, as well as being the turnoff for Hawk's Cay Resort and the small, well-hidden island community of Duck Key. Unless he was sadly mistaken, he would find Mac there.

His cell phone rang as the bus pulled to a stop, and he answered the "Unknown" caller as he ascended the steps.

"Hello, Dr. Ghostwalker. This is Jeremy Ortez. We were quite surprised to get your letter, and the hiring committee is very anxious to interview you. Tomorrow, if that's possible? There's an open ticket waiting for you at Miami International, and once you confirm a flight, we'll have a car waiting for you on this end."

John put his hand on the bus driver's shoulder, motioned for him to reopen the door, and stepped back onto the sidewalk. After assuring Jeremy he would be there, John called a cab and headed back in the direction from which he had just come. He snapped a picture of the Departures sign at MCI as the cab drove under it, and texted the shot to Mac along with the words "waylaid. sorry." He just had to hope she'd still be there in Duck Key a day or two later.

His third and fourth airplane flights were easier than the two before, but he still missed having Katie Lopez as a traveling companion. The limos were minivans this time around, but he actually found that far more relaxing, and he arrived back in Miami feeling like, finally, he might actually be back on the right track to his dream, his destiny, whatever Grandmother Renee might call it. Maybe it was a "four directions of the wind" thing, calling him to renewal. This time when he stepped onto the Keys bus in Homestead, he took a seat and enjoyed the ride, snapping pictures and sending each to Mac as he island-hopped his way south. The two mile walk from the bus stop on US 1, past the entrance to Hawk's Cay Resort, and on to Mac's squat house on Yacht Club Island took John across three narrow hump-backed bridges that crossed over the Venice-like canals which separated each island from the next. He couldn't resist pausing atop each of them, drinking in the view of backyard swimming pools, expensive fishing boats, and even a yacht or two.

Nearly at the end of Yacht Club Island, John turned right off East Seaview Drive onto Jasmine Street, then left onto East Seaview Circle, and finally right into Mac's driveway. The Mini-Cooper wasn't there, so he tried the door. It was locked. John was hot, tired, but happy as a clam. He sat down in the shady doorway, took out his sketch pad, and began drawing the classic island house across the street, with its stately Bahaman shutters and its stunning tropical landscaping. An hour later, his not-quite-so-happy-inner-clam was getting hungry and thirsty, and needed to relieve itself, so John walked around back and tried the sliding door by the swimming pool. That door was also locked. After taking a drink from the garden hose, he stripped down to his boxers, threw his pack and his clothes onto a pile of brightly colored pool noodles, and jumped in for a quick swim and a very refreshing pee. He was climbing up the pool ladder when he heard Mac's car come up the driveway out front. His sense of joy turned suddenly into horror at the sound of excited children exiting the car, the slamming of four very solid sounding car doors, and a mother's voice shouting "Bathroom first, all of you, *then* the pool!"

John swept up his belongings and burst through the north hedge into the next door neighbor's backyard, and hurriedly struggled into his clothes. After deciding no one was coming out of that house to chase him off, he tried to look as if he belonged as he walked around front and back to the street. The clam was feeling pretty depressed as John walked west down Coco Plum Street, past the corner house he'd been sketching, trying to decide what to do next. He thought he heard a door open to his right, but concentrated on looking casual and pressed on.

"Incontinence problems? A lot of us retirees down here struggle with that, so don't you think a thing about it."

John looked down to see that his soaking wet boxers had darkened his blue jeans, front and back, but it was the voice that made him turn back towards the yellow house on his right. A blue and white Mini-Cooper was parked in the shade underneath the stilt house, and Mac was standing in the open doorway smiling at him.

"Apparently the bank found a renter while I was away," she said, pointing to the house around the corner. "Guess I fixed it up a little too well!"

"You might have told me," John said as he walked up the drive.

"Well, yes," Mac said, placing a leather necklace over his head, "but it's just one of those things I love most about you."

John studied the polished circular piece of exotic wood through which the string of leather ran, and puzzled over the stylized engraving on the front. It was just four letters long: "TUIT."

"What is it that you love most about me?" he said looking up at Mac.

"I love that you always get *around to it* eventually."

"Very funny. A round tuit. I always wanted one of these."

They wrapped their arms around each other and kissed like they meant it.

"I missed you," Mac said.

"Me too. You got a long term lease on this place?"

"No," Mac said. "It's a pity too. The owners live in Oklahoma City, and they'll probably be back down next month. I hear they sold their dry cleaning business there."

"Then it's probably not a good time to tell you that I sublet your apartment to Rachel."

"Not to worry," Mac said. "I've got it covered. Come out back."

Behind the house, past the pool and the Tiki-hut, two brand new sailboats were tied to the seawall on the canal. Both were painted blue and white like the Mini-Cooper, and their names were hand painted near the sterns. The bigger of the two was called "Sanctuary I," and the smaller was "Sanctuary II."

"I don't know anything about sailing," John said.

"That's why you get the little one. But fear not, give me a month and I'll make a first rate sailor out of you. Down below," Mac said, boarding the larger boat and opening the cabin hatch, "they've got hot and cold water, a bathroom with a shower, mini-kitchen, A/C, heat, stereo, the works."

"What's the RK mean?" John asked as he ducked below

the boom where the mainsail cover said "Hake Seaward 46RK."

"Retractable Keel. See that switch?" Mac said pointing behind him towards the cockpit. "That controls a winch that raises and lowers the heavily ballasted keel. The draft can be anywhere between two and a half and seven and a half feet."

"Ah," said John as he stepped into the cabin, "I'm sure that will mean something eventually."

They sat across from one another at the small table and neither spoke for several long moments.

"I just couldn't do it," Mac said finally. "Too long around so many people, and I just get, well, you know."

"I do know," John said. "You taught me how to see it and begin to honor it in myself. By the way, will that 32RK fit on a trailer?"

"Sure. The trailer's in storage over at the Duck Key Marina. Why?"

"Well, how would you feel about sort of a bi-coastal relationship? We can keep your boat here in the Keys, and mine near my new part time job. We can go back and forth as often as we want."

"We can do absolutely anything we want," Mac said.

A month later, the *Sanctuary II* rocked gently in its slip off the west coast of Clinton Lake as Mac finished up her web search and started an email to the boat's designer, Nick Hake. She had located two talented fiberglass guys for Nick to interview at his factory in Stuart, Florida, and was passing on their resumes. She was interrupted by a phone call.

"Hello, Mac? Sorry to have to be the messenger again, but your dad never made it through his first month in the federal lock-up. He was stabbed repeatedly with a sharpened toothbrush and he bled out. I'm very sorry."

"What goes around comes around, Oscar," Mac said. "It couldn't have happened to a nicer man."

"I hear you, but I'm afraid there's even more bad news. You're his only heir, Mac."

"Oh shit! How much do I have to get rid of this time, Oscar?"

"Well, between his money, and the money he never signed back over to the Baltimore mob, it might be upwards of a hundred million dollars."

After a few seconds of thoughtful silence, Mac responded: "OK, Oscar, I've decided I can forego shooting the messenger—this time—but guess who's in charge of giving it all away this time?"

"Thank you, Mac. I would be honored. Talk to you soon."

★ ★ ★

Back in town, John stood in the front of a rag-tag group of would-be architects and couldn't quite wipe the smile off his face as he began speaking. "Ladies and gentlemen, welcome to History of Architecture. Here at Haskell, you'll find that our idea of history is a bit more inclusive than it is at most schools, and our views on architecture will focus as much on what some artists might call "the soul" of a building as they do on its form. We do not believe that a structure has a soul in the sense that a living being does, but there certainly can be a spirit of power and of history, for example. Consider the building we occupy right now. It was built by Native American students many generations ago. Here in this place, I like to think that our spirits commune with theirs in some way. As architects, you will decide what, if any spirit speaks through what you create. It is an awesome responsibility, and in order to build into the future, we must understand, and honor, and even cherish the significance of our past."

– The Ghostwalker File –

# Epilogue

SANDY'S Candies & Shack Shop, bayside in San Francisco, is something of an iconic mystery. Locals will tell you that it's always been there, a handy kiosk that caters to the lunch crowd and the tourists alike. Regulars will point out that the little shack always looks like it could fall down at any moment, but never does. Extremely astute regulars might add that the name seems to change with some regularity, and that just about the time they feel like they've gotten to know the owner, someone else takes over. If you look closely, the S in SANDY'S was clearly painted in recently, and more than a few less astute regulars still call the new guy with the perfectly trimmed white beard "Andy."

On a balmy June evening, while Sandy was cleaning up the grill after serving his final burger of the day and saying goodnight to his last customer, a couple strolled up to the counter. Even with his back to the window, Sandy heard their footsteps.

"I'm closed for the day," he said without turning

around, "and the grill's down, but if you want a drink or some chips or candy before I close the window, I'll be right with you."

"That's OK," replied one of the two men, "we just stopped by to say hello, and to see if you wanted to go out for a drink. Our treat."

Sandy froze. He knew that voice because he'd heard it before, and hearing it again was not likely a good thing. He turned around slowly, almost as if there was a gun to his back.

"You look great, Sandy!" Seth Lowenstein said with a smile. "I like the beard. How's life been treating you?"

"OK 'till now. What the hell do you want?"

"I said I wanted to buy you a drink, and I do. By the way, this is my friend, Bernie, but I think you two have already met. Bernie and I are on vacation, and thought we'd check up on you, so come on, lighten up and have a drink with us."

"Do I have a choice?"

"Yes, of course you do. You're a free man now, and whether you know it or not, you did a good thing for some very good people."

"And you're buyin'?" Sandy said as he turned back to finish cleaning the grill.

"I am," Seth said, nudging Bernie and drawing his attention to the sparkly Canadian crutch standing in the corner of the kiosk.

"Well then, as long as I can open my own beer this time, I guess it's OK. Just let me lock up and I'll be right with you."

"That's great, Sandy," Seth laughed. "By the way, have you ever thought about adoption?"

"Adoption? Hell, I don't know. Why?"

"Well," Seth said, "there's this Italian-American kid who's jammed up pretty bad, and he could sure use a role model and a mentor right about now."

"Anybody I know?" Sandy asked, turning around.

Seth pointed his thumb back across the street.

"Is that Joey Beans?" Sandy said squinting. "What the

hell have you gotten me into this time?"

"Who knows?" Seth said. "Let's go figure it out over a beer."

## The End

– Kevin Robinson –

# About the Author

Kevin Robinson is a C6/C7 quadriplegic freelance writer/photographer, novelist, and grandfather of five who thought he had retired to the Florida Key years ago. Instead, it turns out writer's can't always retire as easily as one might think. From 1984 to 2004 Robinson had over 100+ magazine bylines and photo credits, a Knight-Ridder syndicated column in the Sunday *Detroit Free Press* called "Disabled in America, " and three "Stick Foster" mystery novels published in hardback by Walker & Company and in paperback by Vivisphere. In 2004, shortly after "retiring" to the Keys, Robinson and his wheelchair were run over in a crosswalk (crossing with the light) by a speeding motorist. His wheelchair and his pelvis were both totaled, but after a long, slow recovery, his writing muse came to find him, and he wrote a new contemporary novel called *The Ghostwalker File*, and a series of children's tales called *The Grandfather and Grandmother Bear Stories*.

Made in the USA
Columbia, SC
16 August 2018